THE BEE'S WALTZ

Also by Mary E. Lowd

THE BEE'S WALTZ

A LABYRINTH OF SOULS NOVEL

BY

MARY E. LOWD

ShadowSpinners Press

Cover art by Josephe Vandel.
Book design by Matthew Lowes.

ShadowSpinners Press
shadowspinnerspress.com

Typeset in
Minion Pro by Robert Slimbach
and IM FELL Double Pica by Igino Marini.
The Fell Types are digitally reproduced
by Igino Marini, www.iginomarini.com.

Learn more about
the Labyrinth of Souls game at
matthewlowes.com/games.

For Alexis

EDITOR'S PREFACE

Dungeon Solitaire: Labyrinth of Souls is a fantasy game for tarot cards, written by Matthew Lowes and Illustrated by Josephe Vandel. In the game you defeat monsters, disarm traps, open doors, and explore mazes as you delve the depths of a dangerous dungeon. Along the way you collect treasure and magic items, gain skills, and gather companions.

Now ShadowSpinners Press is publishing this and other stand-alone novels inspired by the game. Each *Labyrinth of Souls* novel features a journey into a unique vision of the underworld.

The Labyrinth of Souls is more than an ancient ruin filled with monsters, trapped treasure, and the lost tombs of bygone kings. It is a manifestation of a mythic underworld, existing at a crossroads between people and cultures, between time and space, between the physical world and the deepest reaches of the psyche. It is a dark mirror held up to human experience, in which you may find your dreams ... or your doom. Entrances to this realm can appear in any time period, in any location. There are innumerable reasons why a person may enter, but it is a place antagonistic to those who do, a place where monsters dwell, with obstacles and illusions to waylay adventurers, and whose very walls can be a force of corruption. It is a haunted place, ever at the edge of sanity.

THE BEE'S WALTZ

THE CELESTIAL FRAGMENTS

BOOK TWO

1

THE PALE YELLOW DAWN BRIGHTENED to cotton candy pink with touches of royal purple and honey orange. The air in the high branches of the oak tree was still chilly, cutting through the silver fur of Witch-Hazel's grand tail, which she'd been using like a blanket. Yet the squirrel could tell it would be a hot day when the sun finished rising.

In spite of the breeze rustling through the oak leaves, making the branch Witch-Hazel had been sleeping on sway pleasantly, she was troubled.

Witch-Hazel still had nightmares about being lost and trapped in a labyrinth deep underground. Dark and stuffy. Nowhere a squirrel belonged. And yet, it broke Witch-Hazel's heart to wake up from the nightmares and find herself surrounded by the swaying, leafy branches of whichever tree she'd spent the night in.

When she was trapped in the dark, twisty passages of the labyrinth, there was still hope her quest would end differently than it actually had. Hope that her heart wouldn't be broken. Hope that a goofy otter, twice her height, with a heart full of sunshine and love wouldn't sacrifice himself to save her. Instead, when she woke, reality set in, and she could no longer pretend. She didn't feel worthy of the sacrifice he'd made.

"What did you dream?" Witch-Hazel sleepily asked her current companion, a bee nestled in the curve of a dusky green oak leaf in the pale dawn light. "Is this tree blessed? Is our quest over?"

She said "our quest," but Witch-Hazel was little more than a tag-along on the bee's quest to find her hive a new tree.

"Nothing," Zwi buzzed, bending her antennae crossly. She was a grumpy ball of yellow-and-black striped fuzz. "I dreamed only of flowers and fields and dancing with the other workers in my hive. A perfectly normal dream."

"No blessing then," Witch-Hazel said bleakly. Yet, she wouldn't know what to do with herself if Zwi were to complete her quest. "We'll find another tree to try."

"We need to find a forest," Zwi said. Her translucent wings flittered, eager to begin flying. "These oak trees, separated by expanses of empty field are no good. The flowers here don't sing to me, and the sun beats down too hard."

The farther Witch-Hazel and Zwi travelled, the more the squirrel wondered how the bee intended to find her way back to her hive in the dying purple dogwood when she found a replacement tree.

Witch-Hazel had no idea where the copse of oak trees she'd grown up in were, or even which direction they were in. She'd become a nomad, unanchored to anything in the world except her insectile friend, and a few impossible dreams.

"Okay," Witch-Hazel said. "We'll look for a forest."

As the air warmed and the sun rose in the sky, Zwi flew in laconic zigs and zags above the parched meadows, and Witch-Hazel followed after her, a streak of silver jumping through the grasses. They stopped at several trees—three more oaks and a stately weeping willow beside a dried out hollow that looked like it had once been a lake—before breaking for lunch in a clover field. But none of the trees called to Zwi. None of them had been blessed by the All-Being.

In the clover field, Zwi nuzzled the white blossoms, burying her triangular face deep in their milky petals, while her fuzzy antennae waved, tracing small contented circles as she drank their nectar.

Witch-Hazel scratched at the dry dirt with her claws to dig up the sparse but tender clover roots. Then she munched on them, mixed with the sweetest young clover stalks she could find. It was a simple lunch, nothing like a fine chef could make from the ingredients, but it was serviceable food for tired travelers.

And Witch-Hazel had become a foot-weary traveler, string-bean thin and hungry most of the time. At least,

their nomadic lifestyle meant she was no longer expected—by anyone, especially herself—to be able to bury
troves of meaty nuts and remember where she'd put them.
The cornerstone of squirrel life. And yet, she'd always been
terrible at keeping track of hidden hordes. She was bad at
being a good squirrel. Instead of finding things, she lost
them.

Witch-Hazel dug up extra clover roots and plucked
more stalks to stuff into the ragged backpack she carried
before they moved on from the clover patch. Over the
course of their travels, the backpack had come to be mostly
empty, except for the blue coat her mother had made her
and a stoppered flask that had once held pear cider made
by one of her sisters. Now she filled the flask with water
whenever she got the chance.

Come noon, the air in the fields they travelled through
crackled with heat, and Witch-Hazel's fur burned on the
back of her neck and ears. The backpack shielded her back
from direct sunlight, but at the cost of trapping sweaty
heat beneath it. The sky blazed blue, aggressively, completely clear of any clouds to soften the heat and brightness. It looked like an ocean—one broad surface, hiding
the depths of the heavens behind it.

Zwi stopped to consult with a line of worker ants
winding through the grass in a loopy trail. They were so
small—even smaller than Zwi herself, who was nearly
small enough to fit in Witch-Hazel's pointed ear. Yet, the

ants were barely as large as Zwi's triangular head. Witch-Hazel would never have thought to stop and talk to them. But Zwi landed on the ground beside their trail, crossed her foremost pair of legs in a stately bow, and said, "Most efficient and communally minded workers, may I beg a moment of your time?"

Most of the ants kept walking, straight forward, oblivious to everything except the ant in front of them; totally ignoring the fuzzy yellow-and-black giantess addressing them. But one stopped. Her carapace was a red so dark that it almost looked black, and her tiny eyes were little more than specks of gleaming obsidian.

The ant's antennae waved, mirroring the way Zwi was waving her own larger antenna. Though the effect was somewhat different, as Zwi's antenna were as long as the ant's entire body.

Witch-Hazel kept a respectful distance, trying not to disturb the ants, as she watched. She strained her ears, but she couldn't hear anything. At first, she thought the ant's voice, emanating from those miniscule mandibles, was simply too quiet for her to make out, but then she realized Zwi and the worker ant must be communicating with the way their antennae waggled, their forelegs waved, and their hind legs stamped and shuffled. They were speaking in dance, and it made for a beautiful, strange, and silent conversation. One Witch-Hazel couldn't understand, nor participate in even if she could learn to understand it. She didn't have enough limbs.

Eventually, the dance ended, and the ant scurried back to the line of her compatriots. She squeezed in between two of the others, breaking and crowding the line, but very quickly, the row of marching ants returned to order. The one who'd stopped to speak with Zwi blended in with the others, indiscernible.

Zwi took to the air again, flew over to Witch-Hazel, and bobbed gently in the breeze, floating in front of her squirrel friend with her translucent wings beating a blur.

"What did you learn?" Witch-Hazel asked, dying of curiosity and desperately telling herself that she wasn't jealous of her friend's secret language, totally inaccessible to a simple mammal with four legs and no antennae.

Zwi landed on Witch-Hazel's shoulder, tiny feet clinging to the strap of the squirrel's knapsack. She buzzed, "The news is bad. The ants are seeking a new home too."

"Why?" Witch-Hazel asked.

"Their nest was taken over by another colony. She says it's the third time they've had to move this summer, and they can't find consecrated ground to rebuild in."

"Consecrated ground ..." Witch-Hazel repeated. "Is that like how you're looking for a tree blessed by the All-Being?"

Zwi lifted off from Witch-Hazel's shoulder and took flight again. The squirrel followed her, leaping through the grasses, waiting for an answer. When the bee finally turned around and spoke again, she bobbed erratically in the air as she said, "My fear … I think … the All-Being has stopped blessing the world. If I hadn't hatched and pupated in a purple dogwood blessed by Her Completeness, I'm not sure I would believe in her …"

"*You saw her,*" Witch-Hazel objected. They both had. They'd seen the All-Being when she had come to claim their dying otter friend and whisk him away to her castle in the heavens, forever out of reach.

"Did we see her?" Zwi asked, hovering in place, disturbingly still in spite of her fluttering wings. "Or did we imagine an end for Fish-Breath less heartbreaking than what really happened? Are we sure we didn't leave him—"

Witch-Hazel cut her off: "Don't you dare. *Don't you dare.*" She could picture his broken body, bleeding from the neck, matting his thick brown fur with fresh, wet, red blood. Abandoned on the stone floor of a cursed church, buried deep underground.

But Fish-Breath wasn't there. They hadn't left him behind.

He had left them. When the All-Being appeared, he had grown feathered brown wings and rose upward in the glow of stained glass windows come to life.

Witch-Hazel looked up at the sky, blue and blazing like a sunbaked ocean. Her otter was up there. Out of reach. Waltzing in the All-Being's arms, just like he'd said he would. She believed.

But she wondered, was the All-Being's castle on the other side of that sheet of blue, entirely hidden from her view? Were its spires and turrets nestled in the creamy, pearly folds of a puffy white cloud, wandering endlessly through the sky? Or were its gleaming walls and balustrades shining fiercely inside the burning gold eye of the sun itself, too bright to look at directly?

Witch-Hazel had held a piece of the sun once in her paws. The Sun Shard had looked like a faceted topaz gemstone, set inside gold formed into the petals of a sunflower in a heavy pendant. The gem had glowed warmly to the touch. She'd been wearing the pendant against her breast when she first met Fish-Breath, hidden beneath her coat, because she'd been afraid the much larger mammal might want to steal it.

When he'd risen up to the heavens, though, his revival had partly been due to the power of the Sun Shard, after she'd placed the pendant lovingly around his neck, gifting it to him.

Strength, flight, and endless breath. Those had been the gifts bestowed by the Celestial Treasures—the Sun Shard, the Star Sliver, and the Moon Opal—each of which she'd carefully collected from where they'd been lost for ages in the dark labyrinths under the earth. She'd intended to use them herself to meet the All-Being, a frivolous desire, she knew now. Instead, she'd used them to save Fish-Breath's life after he'd succumbed to the attacks of vicious, angry zombies controlled by a sorcerous snake.

Witch-Hazel fought back tears at the memory of Fish-Breath's fall, and through the blur in her eyes, she saw a flash in the distance. Moments later, a rumbling crack sounded. There were clouds, she noticed, at the fringes of the sky. Hovering far away at the very edge of the horizon, lumpy gray storm clouds lumbered into the sea of blue, shading the land below.

But their cooling shade wasn't enough.

Witch-Hazel's nose twitched. She could already smell the sizzling scent of fire wafting in the breeze. Bright orange sparks drifted lazily through the air above them.

Birds flew past, winging as fast as they could, hurrying and cawing, "Run! Run! Everyone run!"

Witch-Hazel didn't wait to consult with Zwi. The bee could fly faster than she could run anyway. So Witch-Hazel ran.

2

FIRE SWEPT ACROSS the grassy plains, lingering over relatively moist clover fields, and then in turn, raging at full rampage speeds through the crackly dry yellow grasses. Witch-Hazel followed the direction of the birds, flying and warning creatures below. She could feel the heat from the sun and the fire that she knew was behind her, but she dared not stop to look back at it.

She wondered what would happen to the marching lines of the ant colony when the fire got to them. They couldn't run like her or fly like Zwi. Witch-Hazel ran until she felt a stitch in her side, and then she kept running.

Heat singed the long, wispy, silver hairs at the end of Witch-Hazel's tail, and she felt panic setting in. Maybe if she stopped there would be an abandoned gopher hole she could hide in ... Would that work? More relevantly, would she even be able to find one? She may be a directionless nomad, fleeing from her own heartbreak, but she didn't want to die. Especially not burned to death.

The air danced around Witch-Hazel as she ran, billowing into mirages from the heat—glimpses of the oak copse where she'd been reared; flickers of the dark passages from the labyrinth under the earth. For a moment, she thought she even caught a glimpse of the fire realm itself, shimmering like flames in her peripheral vision. Or maybe it was simply the fire, catching up to her.

Witch-Hazel's eyes stung from the dry heat and the hazy smoke beginning to fill the air. And also, maybe, a few tears of regret.

The queen of the fire realm, a salamander named Amalah, had once invited Witch-Hazel to become her hand-maiden there. But Witch-Hazel had refused the offer, and the salamander queen wasn't here now to reiterate it. An expired invitation would not protect Witch-Hazel from burning like the grass around her, scorching the bottoms of her paws.

As Witch-Hazel began to despair, a new mirage appeared to taunt her, promising her eyes the cool shade of a thick forest. Straight ahead. Exactly the kind of forest Zwi had been hoping for—filled with trees of every kind, so many trees that they choked out the hot sunlight, making a world all their own underneath their branches, nearly as dark as the labyrinth had been. But bursting with life—buzzing insects, skittering rodents, perfumed flowers, and moist, springy loam—instead of laying fallow with dead dirt and dried up roots.

Witch-Hazel knew better than to believe in mirages, but her sides hurt; her legs ached; her paws stung; her eyes were watering; and she was running straight toward the tempting mirage anyway.

Perhaps she was looking at a magical realm akin to the fire realm. A forest realm.

As Witch-Hazel reached the edge of the forest and felt the cool shade fall over her back, she saw another flash and then heard another rumbling crack from behind. This time, she risked coming to a stop, turning, and looking back at the sky.

The unmarred sheet of blue had been totally lost behind roiling gray clouds, tumultuous, and streaming across the sky under the power of a strong wind. The orange flames of the fire licking their way across the dry fields were mostly hidden underneath the billowing blankets of pungent smoke pouring off of them. They peeked out like tiny devils, checking on the progress of their work.

Witch-Hazel drew a deep breath, scented with the moist, earthy smell of loam and sweet touches of honeysuckle and lavender. The forest was real. At least, it seemed to be. And the trees held the air under them in their branches, close and safe, protected from the smoke. Would it be enough? Or would the forest burn too?

It would burn. Of course it would burn. Witch-Hazel's ears twisted and twitched, listening for any clue of a direction to take, somewhere that might be safe. Somewhere that could protect her and Zwi, but all she heard was the buzzing of her friend, flying erratically between the pillars of the tree trunks, seemingly searching as much as she was.

Witch-Hazel looked up at the canopy of interwoven branches, rich with leaves that would burst into fans of flame on skeletal veins when the fire got here. Then the veins would burn too.

Witch-Hazel would move faster in the canopy, and Zwi could fly that high.

Zwi … could fly higher.

As a bee, Zwi could fly above the fire entirely, wait it out, and abandon Witch-Hazel to burn.

The squirrel's heart beat faster. She leapt toward the nearest tree, scrambled straight up the broad pine trunk until she reached the highest branches, and then began the complicated, springy dance native to her own people, jumping from one branch to another, treating a forest worth of trees as a single entity. Below, the forest might seem to separate out into individual trunks; but from above, any squirrel knew the truth: they were all one interlocking being.

But not to Zwi. The bee was searching for one tree; a single home for her hive. Deep in her heart, Witch-Hazel knew it was a fool's errand. The All-Being hadn't blessed any of these trees. That was clear from the way they were bursting into flame behind her; the fire licking its way through the path Witch-Hazel had taken, as if it were following her particularly.

Queen Amalah had once told Witch-Hazel that squirrels were creatures of fire. Witch-Hazel didn't know about that … but the fire was doing a disturbingly good impression, as it followed her, of being a bright red-orange squirrel.

Another flash; ahead of Witch-Hazel this time; and bright enough to stop her in her tracks, clinging to the needled pine bough where she happened to be.

A rumbling crack.

Witch-Hazel's breath caught as it occurred to her that if the fire came burning through the forest from both directions, she'd have nowhere left to go. She looked up again, this time only a few stray branches blocked her view of the storm cloud strewn sky. She could imagine Fish-Breath up there, swimming through the clouds with his big feathery wings, just like an otter swimming through the depths of a lake. But more celestial. Exactly as he should be. She wanted to leap off the branch and rise up through the sky, sprouting silvery feathered wings of her own, and join him in dancing among the purple-edged gray clouds.

But there was no otter in the sky.

And she had no wings.

The only direction she could go was down.

Zwi appeared, hovering before her, bobbing about frantically between the brushy boughs. She buzzed, "I found a lake."

"A lake?" Witch-Hazel could hide from the flames in the cool water of a lake.

"Follow me."

The bee descended through the forest canopy, zigging around branches, and zagging around tree trunks. Witch-Hazel followed as best as she could, claws scraping and sliding against the tree bark. She felt suddenly clumsy in her own arboreal realm. But then her paws were sore and tired; her head ached from the smoke; her eyes were bleary and watering; and she wasn't used to choosing her path by way of following an erratic honeybee.

Four paws hit the ground at once, and Witch-Hazel's tail arched into a perfect flowing curve. A tiny silver waterfall. She was a self-contained fountain in the midst of a parched forest, dying for want of water. The loam felt disturbingly warm under Witch-Hazel's paw pads, but then the warmth could have simply been the tingling numbness that had been growing throughout her body, everywhere except the back of her head, behind her left ear, where a headache pulsed like a knife slicing into her brain. It was the only thing she could feel clearly.

"Come, come," Zwi buzzed, circling around the squirrel to get her attention.

Dizzily, Witch-Hazel took off after Zwi as soon as the bee began flying straight, etching a line through the underbrush of fern, blackberry brambles, oxalis, and dry bracken that would burst into flames far too easily when the fire got to it.

The trees and underbrush came right up to the edge of the crystal bright lake, so Witch-Hazel nearly stumbled into the water. Steam rose off the surface, evaporating as the hot wind from the forest blew over the lake. The water stretched far enough in every direction that Witch-Hazel wouldn't be able to swim all the way across. She wasn't very practiced at swimming. There'd been a small babbling brook near the oak copse where she'd grown up, and she'd splashed in the shallow water with her littermates, hopping from one round river rock to another. Mostly trying to avoid getting wet. But that wasn't swimming.

Perhaps there was a large branch nearby that she could float on the water? She could cling to it like a boat. Frantically, Witch-Hazel looked around, but she saw nothing she could use. She heard the quiet, shushing roar of the fire growing closer, and it cast a nightmarish light, dim and red, shining up and out from the forest, when light was meant to stream downward from the sky.

Looking back at the lake, Witch-Hazel's ears flattened in consternation. She had no choice. She dove into the lake.

Paddling with her paws, she felt the water stream uselessly between her paw pads. And her glorious flag of a tail diminished to a long, narrow whip with the fur wetted down, worthless for steering. She wished for webbed paws and a thick rudder tail like Fish-Breath's. She wished for Fish-Breath to appear in a puff of purple sparkly magic and carry her through the water in his strong arms, maybe beat his magical wings and fly high above the forest, carrying her into the sky.

Instead, she paddled hard with her tired legs, struggling to keep her head over the surface, slowly losing ground, and feeling her chin splash into the water, filling her mouth with choking, gagging gulps of unwanted liquid that she sputtered on and tried to cough out.

"Oh, patience and complexity of the All-Being ... I'm drowning," she gasped. Or thought. The words didn't come together around the water gurgling into her mouth.

Witch-Hazel's last glimpse of the surface burned with the reflected glow of the forest fire—orange and deadly, flickering doubly from the broken, choppy, ripples caused by Witch-Hazel's struggles to swim. Then her head went under, and her wavery view of the hot air was replaced by the wavery view of an underwater world. From underneath, the glow of the fire looked much calmer, blurred by the ripples and smoothed by the bending of the light.

One mirage replaced another.

Life was nothing but a series of mirages, and Witch-Hazel wanted no part of it. Her lungs burned, and she was tempted to open her mouth and let the water fill them.

A sense of profound calmness overcame the squirrel, and her body relaxed into floating downward. This was somewhere Fish-Breath would love to be—the clear water of the lake was beautiful. It was almost supernaturally clear, and she could see all the way to the bottom, many tree heights down. It was like she was floating down through crystal. Far beneath her, in the middle of the lake, the black skeletal branches of a fossilized tree reached upward, stretching toward the surface without reaching it.

Fishes swam around and between the tree's leafless boughs like they were birds. Trout with green and magenta stripes slipped through the water like tiny slices of rainbow that had lost their way and fallen down from the sky.

Then one of the tree's branches seemed to break off from the higher boughs of the tree, closest to Witch-Hazel; a smear of darkness streaked through the water toward her. As it got closer, Witch-Hazel's bleary eyes made out the round shapes of a wide nose, bright eyes, and tiny ears. An otter swam toward Witch-Hazel, and he looked so much like Fish-Breath it made her heart hurt.

The otter swam a curlicue like a question mark when he arrived at her and held out a luminous white flower with angular, geometrically pleasing petals in one paw. A water lily. As if drawn to him, Witch-Hazel reached out her own paw, and the otter helped her clasp the flower, curling her fingers around its stem. His webbed paw wrapped around her paw.

He looked like Fish-Breath. She wanted him to be Fish-Breath. Her heart hurt, but eerily, her lungs stopped aching.

Witch-Hazel looked at the flower.

The luminous geometry of the petals mesmerized her—triangular tips arranged in descending, overlapping circles—and the stamens in the middle glowed with a soft yellow light.

The otter spoke, bubbles streaming up from his mouth, catching in the net of his whiskers: "The flower lets you breathe. It's an air lily. Don't let it go." He flipped around in a fluid motion, spine bending like a horseshoe. Still holding Witch-Hazel's paw, he swam down toward the skeletal branches of the black tree, pulling her through the water after him, faster than she could possibly swim with her squirrel paws and squirrel tail, even if she knew how to swim.

3

THE MYSTERIOUS OTTER brought Witch-Hazel to the stony boughs of the fossilized tree, so far under the surface of the lake that Witch-Hazel doubted she could get back up on her own, even with the magical power of the air lily letting her breathe.

Witch-Hazel reached out to touch the tree as she floated past. Its dark bark was hard against the pads of her free paw—ungiving. Nothing she'd be able to sink her claws into and climb. She wouldn't be able to cling to this tree's bark and skitter safely through its branches. Instead her claws would bounce off the hard crenulated surface.

For although the tree-thing was shaped like a tree, the life and spirit of a tree had clearly left it long ago, many squirrel lifetimes ago. The tree-thing was a rock, poorly imitating a tree. A grave marker where a tree had once been. Nothing more.

Yet, being underwater, Witch-Hazel supposed she could float beside the branches, grabbing at them for guidance. An imitation of climbing to go with an imitation of a tree. Although, its highest branches were still upsettingly far below the surface of the lake.

The otter continued pulling Witch-Hazel downward, following the path of the tree-thing's trunk. Here and there, more of the air lilies bloomed, glowing cheerfully. Their green vines—very much alive, in contrast to the tree-thing itself—wrapped around the branches and trunk, clinging to its stony bark. Their light illuminated dark green algae growing on the trunk, as well as lines of honey-orange sap dripping down the trunk's crevasses, forming tear drop shaped beads, like wax dripping down the sides of a candle.

Witch-Hazel reached out to the honey-colored sap and found it was hard too. Also stone, but softer stone than the tree-thing's trunk. Something else that had died and hardened long ago. But its surface was satiny, instead of rough like granite.

"It's amber," the otter said. "And it remembers what the rest of the world has forgotten."

Witch-Hazel was fascinated as the otter guided her with his webbed paws to face an old knot-hole near the base of the tree, only a few feet above the silty floor of the lake. Disturbed by their swimming, silt rose up from beneath them in dusty clouds.

The otter pointed at the knot-hole and said, "Watch."

The hole was large enough to have held a perfect squirrel's nest, but it had been entirely filled in with the honey-gold stone forming a perfect oval of amber.

The oval of amber embedded in the knot-hole in the tree-thing's trunk was so smooth, she could see the shadow of her silver reflection in its warm gold surface. She could also see past the surface—bubbles and granules that had been trapped in the sap before it hardened stayed suspended now in the amber, giving it texture and complexity. The orange, honey, and gold colors shifted through the oval of amber, like the folds in cake batter as its being mixed.

Witch-Hazel remembered one time when her mother had baked a birthday cake, made from ground nuts and honey, for her and her littermates. All her sisters, brothers, and herself had loved the sweet cake, frosted with a paste made from flower petals and mint leaves.

But Witch-Hazel's favorite part had been watching her mother mix the ingredients, working magic as she combined simple foods to make more complex ones. Perhaps that's why Witch-Hazel had been so entranced by Fish-Breath when she'd met him. He'd been a wizard of a chef, able to take scraps saved in her backpack and whip up mouth-watering soups and stews. Like her mother. Unlike herself.

As Witch-Hazel remembered watching her mother mix the cake batter, she began to imagine she could see the memory, replaying, inside the honeyed folds of amber. And then … she realized she wasn't imagining anything.

The vision was there, playing for her, like a dream spread across the amber.

"How …" she started to ask, but when she looked for the otter, he was no longer there.

Witch-Hazel was floating beside the tree-thing's trunk, deep beneath the surface of a lake, clinging to a magic flower to breathe. All alone. She looked at the oval of amber again. The vision of her mother mixing cake batter had disappeared.

In its place, Witch-Hazel saw a vision of the All-Being, staring out at her with mis-matched eyes, uneven ears, one antler and one horn, dozens of different kinds of tails, and wings of every sort—an amalgam of all animals, all their best traits, combined into one all-encompassing being.

Wings, tails, hooves, paws, horns; feathers, fur, scales, and skin. Asymmetrical yet balanced. Progenitor to all the creatures in the world.

The sight took Witch-Hazel's breath away, a feeling that frightened her deep under a lake. She coughed, sputtered, and almost missed the vision of the All-Being winking at her (or had she imagined that?) before turning and walking away into the foyer of a castle.

The castle was exactly how Witch-Hazel would have imagined it—spires, towers, turrets—all made from shining gold, and settled lightly on the cottony surface of a perfect, puffy, white cloud. Water fell from the cloud, too thick and constant to be rain. It was a waterfall.

The vision pulled back, and Witch-Hazel could see the majestic silver waterfall stretch with frothy white water at its edges all the way from the castle in the sky, down to the surface of the Earth. It was the endless river Fish-Breath and his beaver friend, Twiggy, had spoken of, the river they'd hoped to restart and sail upon, up into the sky.

The vision pulled back further, and Witch-Hazel saw more waterfalls, more endless rivers, looping between the ground and the clouds; trees and vines also stretched all the way up from the earth to the heavens. The realms of earth and air were tied together in a complicated network of interwoven rivers and vines. It was beautiful.

The vision zoomed back in, focused tightly on the castle. The All-Being sat on a throne, and four figures approached her. Witch-Hazel recognized two of them—Amalah, the salamander queen of the fire realm, and Kokeu, the koi fish queen of the water realm. Witch-Hazel had met both of them before—they'd aided her during her quest beneath the earth.

The other two figures were a butterfly with richly patterned, rainbow wings, and a brown mouse, wearing a carefully tailored suit of dusky, royal purple and a golden crown settled between his round ears.

Each of the four bowed before the All-Being. The koi fish bowed her head from within a puddle of glowing water, like a flat portal to her own realm, that seemed to magically follow her, letting her move through the castle as easily as the others with their wings and legs.

With every movement of the butterfly's wings, light shining through their intricate patterns cast rainbows on the walls of the castle foyer. The salamander's glistening skin, a rich shade of maroon, dripped with flames as she moved. And tiny green leaves and shoots seemed to spring from the ground under the mouse's paws wherever he stepped, whether it be on hard stone or the cottony down of the clouds.

The mouse took the gold crown from between his ears and held it elegantly against his breast as he bowed. After their bows, the four royal creatures danced together, waltzing to music Witch-Hazel couldn't hear. The koi fish's puddle swirled into a vortex; the butterfly whirled up eddies of wind with her wings; and the mouse and salamander twirled in each others' arms. They were all such tiny gods—only the koi fish was bigger than a squirrel.

Witch-Hazel lost track of time as she watched the comings and goings of the tiny queens and one king in the All-Being's castle. Years seemed to pass within the vision— celebrations of midsummer and deep winter feasts marked the passing of the seasons as the vision sped through many lifetimes' worth of years.

Other denizens of the different realms came to the balls, sailing up through the sky on giant ships with white muslin sails that billowed like flags as their boats slid sideways along the waterfalls, as if the falling water were a part of a normal river, running horizontally along the world.

Boats sailed up and down the waterfall rivers; cities sprung up, woven into the branches of extremely tall trees and the tangles of vines that grew all the way from the ground up to the All-Being's castle in the clouds.

And then the cities began to dwindle.

Trees died and fell over.

Vines shriveled up and withered away.

The waterfalls diminished from gushing rivers to silvery trickles. Eventually, they dried up entirely, becoming only erratic rainfall. The age of the sailing ships was no more.

Inside the foyer of the castle, the three queens and one king seemed to quarrel, although Witch-Hazel could only see their expressions—angry faces, gesticulating limbs—and not hear their words. The All-Being watched from her throne, ears of different sizes twitching, and various tails swishing. Eventually, she reached with an arm—bare-skinned like a human's—and pointed, seemingly banishing the tiny queens and king from her castle.

The mouse threw his crown to the floor and stomped away, tail drooping and dragging along the ground, leaving a trail of green sprouts in his wake. The koi fish somersaulted in her puddle, and the mystical pool of water seemed to swallow itself, disappearing as if Queen Kokeu had never been there at all.

The salamander disappeared in a puff of dark gray smoke, but the butterfly lingered, flapping her wings—like stained-glass windows with their brilliant colors—slowly and sadly, hovering before the All-Being's throne. Eventually, she landed at the All-Being's feet—a golden lion's paw, gigantic next to the tiny butterfly, and a cloven hoof. The butterfly bent her six strangely-jointed legs, bowing before the All-Being in profound genuflection, but the All-Being's human-like hand pointed toward the castle's gates again. Uncompromising. Unwavering. And finally, the butterfly flew away, leaving the castle to rise among the clouds like a soap bubble—colorful, ethereal, and infinitely delicate.

Then the amber went dark.

Witch-Hazel's ears flattened in consternation. Why had the deities fought? What had caused the endless rivers to dry up? The vision in the amber had told her a story, but she only understood part of what she had seen. Too much was missing.

Witch-Hazel turned and twisted, awkwardly rotating herself as she floated, looking for the otter. But he was still gone. And she was alone at the bottom of a lake, clinging to a glowing, magical flower.

With a sigh, Witch-Hazel realized she would need to find her way back up to the surface of the lake on her own.

She considered traveling along the silty floor of the lake beneath her instead, but there were so many rocks and plants to obscure the way. She feared she could wander the bottom of the lake, lost for days. No, she needed to swim back to the surface where she'd be able to see her way to the lake's edge, and where her friend Zwi could have a chance of finding her.

She couldn't wait to tell Zwi about the vision. The bee knew so much more lore about the All-Being than Witch-Hazel did, perhaps she could make more sense of what the amber had showed her.

Witch-Hazel writhed in the water, trying to move herself the way that the otter had, and slowly, her movements started to sort themselves out and make more sense. If she moved her arms together, as if she were trying to pull herself forward, and kicked her feet, she could get herself moving. Her whip-like tail wasn't as useful as a thick rudder, but swaying it the right way helped her orient herself. Soon, she was swimming up along the trunk of the tree at a reasonable pace—albeit painfully slow compared to an otter. She was able to gain some speed by kicking and pulling at the tree-thing's branches as she passed them, using it a little like a large, eerie ladder.

As Witch-Hazel swam along, she paused here and there to pluck more of the air lilies from where they grew on the tree-thing's trunk. She kept the first lily that the otter had given her in her paw, but she stuffed the others into her backpack. They might be useful later.

Witch-Hazel also noticed a particularly beautiful bead of amber bulging out from its crevasse in the tree-thing's bark far enough that she thought, maybe, she could break the bead off. With a bit of scrambling, she managed to wedge her claws between the bead and the crevasse, and the narrow line of amber leading down to the bead cracked.

Witch-Hazel held the honey-colored, teardrop shaped stone in her paw, marveling at its beauty. She gazed at the satiny curve of its surface and wondered what memories it might contain … Or were the memories contained by the tree-thing itself? She didn't know, but she hoped the amber bead might eventually offer her more visions if she took it with her and continued to gaze at it. For now, she tucked it into a small hidden pocket where it would be safe in her backpack, and she continued swim-climbing the tree-thing upward.

4

When Witch-Hazel reached the topmost branch of the tree-thing, she had to let go of the security it had provided her. She felt like she was jumping off the top of a tree and into the sky, hoping to float up to the clouds instead of crashing down to the earth.

But underwater, that worked. And since she'd developed a rhythm that worked for swimming—an awkward, bumbling rhythm—she kept ascending toward the disturbing orange light of the lake's surface.

Witch-Hazel wondered if this experience would affect her dreams. Now that her body knew what it felt like to fly up from the top of a tree, would she dream about doing the same thing, but above water? Would she dream about flying into the sky and seeing Fish-Breath? Instead of only seeing him in dreams filled with darkness and fear and bleeding necks ...

Witch-Hazel wondered as she swam what had happened to the otter who'd led her down to the amber pane in the trunk of the tree-thing. He'd disappeared so completely that she couldn't help questioning whether he'd been a vision as well. Or perhaps … and she could barely let herself think about this … a visitation.

He had looked so much like Fish-Breath.

Could the otter have been Fish-Breath? Sending her a vision, trying to tell her something? Trying to teach her something that she needed to know in order to find her way up to him in the sky?

Witch-Hazel kept pulling herself toward the surface, feeling the water stream between her paw pads, and replaying the vision she'd seen of the All-Being's realm over and over again in her mind. She tried to notice any detail that might be the key to why the mysterious otter—who she was increasingly sure must have been Fish-Breath—had brought her down to see it.

And she kept returning to one image: as the waterfalls had dried up, and the trees had fallen over, and the thick green vines had withered away to cracking, brittle strands of yellow straw-like detritus that blew away like dust in the wind … One vine had remained. As she'd watched the vision unfold in the amber, Witch-Hazel had assumed the remaining vine would meet the same fate as all the other paths up to the All-Being's castle in the clouds.

But what if it hadn't?

What if there was still one vine left that tied the earth to the heavens?

And now, Witch-Hazel had the magical air lilies that would let her keep breathing as she climbed through the thin air at its heights. Maybe she could make it to Fish-Breath after all. Maybe she had a quest of her own.

Witch-Hazel's head broke the surface of the lake, and she gasped, gulping deeply at the true air. Her lungs filled, and she coughed at the spicy smokiness. But it felt good to breathe real air—not just the mystical air from the air lilies—again.

Floating at the surface of the lake, treading water in a way she'd never known was possible before, Witch-Hazel marveled at how much easier it is to swim when one isn't panicking about drowning. In a similar vein, she found the inferno blazing around the edges of the lake much less frightening now that she had the lake's cool water to protect her from its flames.

Slowly, Witch-Hazel dogpaddled toward the nearest shore. The thick undergrowth was gone, and the dark loam steamed with the passing heat from the fire that had moved on. She could still see the flames in the distance, and raging beside the far side of the lake. On the closer side, the trunks of the trees were all scorched, black with ash and denuded of their leaves, making them look a little like the tree-thing at the bottom of the lake.

As she swam, Witch-Hazel passed tiny flotillas of leaves, repurposed as lifeboats for crowds of ants, spiders, and even flying insects who must have grown tired of flying and needed somewhere to rest until the forest fire passed.

Zwi must be floating on a leaf somewhere, Witch-Hazel thought. Surely, her friend would come find her. Zwi travelled much faster and sensed much farther with her delicate attunement to the vibrations in the world than Witch-Hazel could.

The squirrel crawled exhaustedly onto the shore, and after resting a while, still clutching the air lily in her paw, she sat up, pulled off her backpack, and began sorting through all the lilies she'd collected. The flowers still glowed, but their light was too dim to notice during daylight if she hadn't already seen them deep under the lake.

Witch-Hazel braided several stems together—using extra vines that had pulled free and come with them as she'd picked the flowers—to make a sort of chain for the first air lily, the one the otter had given her. She made the braid long enough to go over her head and was settling the flower on her breast as Zwi came flying to her.

"I knew you'd survive," Zwi buzzed. Her tone betrayed the lie in her words—she'd been worried about Witch-Hazel, perhaps too worried to risk giving into the feeling and showing it. The bee landed on one of the spare air lilies that laid strewn beside Witch-Hazel's backpack. "These are pretty."

"They're more than pretty," Witch-Hazel said, gently touching her claw tips to the pointed ends of the petals. "These are air lilies. They saved me from drowning."

Zwi's antennae rotated in a way that displayed interest, without committing to belief.

"Really," Witch-Hazel said. "I was sinking, deep beneath the surface, drowning and then—" She wasn't sure she wanted to tell Zwi about the otter. His presence had been too strange and fantastical—more so than the air lilies themselves, which she could prove were real. The otter seemed more like the invention of an unhinged mind and lovesick heart. So, she skipped past him. "—I found these flowers, and I could breathe again."

Skeptically, Zwi picked up the smallest of the lilies—still larger than her, but light enough for her to lift it—and dragged the flower, stem trailing on the ground, over to the lapping water of the lake. She dropped the flower, petal-side down, and landed on it. She then crawled to the flower's underside, disappearing into the cluster of petals under the mirrored surface of the lake. A few moments later, she emerged, antennae vibrating excitedly. "That is amazing. In all my travels, and all the dances I've watched of others' travels from my hive, I have never heard of a flower like this before."

Tentatively, almost afraid to say the words, Witch-Hazel suggested, "It would let us breathe in the heights of the sky … if we were to, you know, journey to the All-Being's castle."

"True," Zwi agreed cautiously, still standing on the back of the upside down, floating flower. "But I cannot fly that high. And you can't fly at all."

"When I was under the water," Witch-Hazel said, "I had a vision of the All-Being."

Zwi held very still. The first bonds of their friendship had been tied when the bee and squirrel had shared a vision from the All-Being, which they chose to keep secret from the others in their traveling band—Fish-Breath and the beaver, Twiggy. A shared secret can be a strong bond. A shared vision is an even stronger one.

Zwi believed in visions.

"What did you see?" the bee asked, her wings fluttering ever so lightly.

Witch-Hazel told Zwi everything—the tree-thing, the amber, the details she'd seen of the comings and goings of the All-Being's court. Everything that is, except about the otter who'd led her to the vision.

Witch-Hazel kept the bewildering, beguiling memory of the mysterious otter who looked like Fish-Breath—so very like Fish-Breath!—for herself.

After finishing her story, Witch-Hazel took out the bead of amber she'd broken off of the tree-thing and showed it to Zwi. The bee stared at it for a very long time, gazing at her reflection in the honey-colored stone. But eventually, she had to admit that she saw nothing. No vision revealed itself.

"I think you're right," Zwi buzzed. "We should look for the remaining vine and climb it to the castle of the All-Being."

"You do?" Witch-Hazel was stunned and overjoyed. She hadn't expected Zwi to agree with her. Especially not so easily.

"Yes, in all our travels, we haven't found a single tree blessed by the All-Being. Not a single one."

"So?" Witch-Hazel assumed that blessed trees were very rare. Thus the difficulty of Zwi's quest and her failure to complete it so far hadn't surprised her.

"There should be blessed trees everywhere. Maybe not suitable ones … Maybe already claimed by other hives, or blessed for other purposes. But the land should be filled with the All-Being's blessings. That's the story the dances passed down in my hive, and the dances we've learned from other hives, tell us."

As Zwi spoke, the storm clouds filling the sky darkened, turning from flat gray to a rich gray made up of navy blues and angry purples. Then the storm broke, and water poured down from the sky. The silver rain was so thick that it was almost like the waterfalls from Witch-Hazel's vision, and it pressed down, unrelentingly, on the flames of the forest fire that still tried, stubbornly, to keep raging on the far side of the lake.

Water from the sky and fire from the earth battled with each other over a middle ground where all the elements met, where all the animals lived, depending on the outcome of skirmish, depending even more on the outcome of the war.

"There should be a balance," Zwi said. "But the balance is broken."

Slowly, the orange flames licked their way down to mere embers, smoking from the ravished forest floor. The rain let up, softening from a deluge, a complete downpour, to mere mist sprinkling over the wounded trees. Then a line of sunbeams broke through a seam in the thick clouds, and although the sky was still dark, the space below the clouds filled with rainbows.

"Have you heard that foxes hold their weddings during weather like this?" Witch-Hazel asked, gazing at the eerie bands of color in the dark sky.

"What?"

Bees would have little reason to care about the comings and goings of foxes. But squirrels do.

"When the sky is filled with both rain and sun—rainbow weather my mother called it—that's when foxes hold their weddings." Witch-Hazel paused, feeling foolish. Defensively, she explained, "It's a story squirrels tell, probably to make kits feel safer right after a storm. The idea is that foxes will be too busy to hunt us, because they're dancing and laughing, marrying each other during the short window while the weather is right."

"It's a pretty legend," Zwi buzzed. She didn't comment on its accuracy. Maybe she didn't know. Probably she didn't care. "So, how do we find the vine? Were there more clues in your vision?"

Witch-Hazel shook her head, flattening her ears. She'd hoped Zwi would have an idea. She was the one who could fly high enough to have a hope of seeing the vine from a distance. She was the one who communed with trees in her sleep.

But it was true that Witch-Hazel had been the one to see the vision.

"I don't remember any clues. I was hoping you'd have an idea." She wrung her paws together and admitted, "Honestly, I was hoping you could just fly up into the sky and see it."

"If I'd ever seen a vine like that, I would have told you," Zwi buzzed.

Witch-Hazel nodded. "I suppose you would have. I guess that means, even if we knew which direction it's in, it must be very far away. Too far to see. That means a long journey."

"Not necessarily ..." Zwi ran a taloned forehand along the length of her right antenna, bending it forward. "Remember the fairy rings that we used to travel from one cave to another underground?"

"The circle of mushrooms?" Witch-Hazel asked excitedly.

"Yes, that's right."

Zwi had inscribed complicated patterns in the air over the circle of speckled, red-capped mushrooms, and her flying dance had caused the mushrooms to teleport them—Zwi, Witch-Hazel, Fish-Breath, and Twiggy altogether—from one part of the giant network of underground tunnels and caverns to another. Instantaneously. As if by magic. Scratch that, clearly by magic.

"There are fairy rings above ground too?" Witch-Hazel asked. "Why haven't we been traveling by them?"

Zwi held up her two foremost arms in a shrug. "There are trees here. I'd hoped they'd be blessed and that there would be no call to travel that far away."

Witch-Hazel thought quietly about that. From her perspective, they'd already traveled very far away from where they'd begun. But then, from what she knew of Zwi and her life back in her hive, it sounded like many bees were used to traveling farther in a single day, gathering pollen from flowers far afield, than most of the squirrels Witch-Hazel had known traveled in an entire lifetime.

If Zwi thought the fairy rings would carry them far away, then it must mean very far. She wondered if the trees and plants would be different. Or the sky. But then, the sky hadn't looked different in her vision. Except for all those waterfalls …

"Of course, we still need to know which direction to travel," Witch-Hazel observed. "Even if the fairy rings can get us there faster."

"Trees and mushrooms talk to each other with their tangled roots," Zwi said. "If anyone knows where this vine grows from, it'll be the community of tangled roots. I don't dance their language, but the keepers of the fairy rings can."

Witch-Hazel felt her excitement rising. "Fairies? They're real?" She hadn't known fairies were real. Somehow, she'd thought "fairy ring" was just a name. But she'd met ghosts, zombies, sorcerers, and the sister of the Sphynx on her travels. Why not fairies too?

"In a way," Zwi said. "They certainly like to think of themselves as fairies."

"How do we find one?"

"First, we find a fairy ring."

Zwi took off, flying through the forest.

Witch-Hazel scrambled to shove all the loose air lilies back into her backpack, and then sling the bag over her shoulders. As quickly as she could, she scurried after the buzzing bee, heart racing now that she was following a quest of her own, and not just tagging along.

5

AFTER A FEW HOURS of travel through the muddy, ashy mess left behind by the forest fire and sudden downpour, the difference between following her own quest and following Zwi's became less clear. Either way, Witch-Hazel continued through the forest, plodding along the scorched loam with weary paws, following a trail blazed by the fuzzy yellow and black bee. But she tried to hold onto the difference in her heart. She tried to believe she'd see Fish-Breath again soon. Though, she tried not to believe too hard ... She didn't want her heart doubly broken.

Following Zwi was easier than usual as they traveled through the burned out parts of the forest—fewer leaves and less underbrush blocked Witch-Hazel's view. Nonetheless, she was relieved when they made it to the edge of the devastation and the undergrowth filled back in with fern fronds, leafy shrubs, and tiny star-like flowers.

Witch-Hazel insisted on stopping to rest for a while at sunset. She climbed the tallest of the nearby trees and sat on one of its highest branches, so she could watch the sky turn gold and pink over the sea of green treetops while munching on the clover stalks and roots she'd saved earlier. She considered nibbling the tip of one of the air lily stalks, but it smelled so sweet, so delicious that Witch-Hazel feared she would find that she wanted to eat them all. And she would need them when they found the vine into the sky.

Better to avoid temptation in the first place than to give in and find the temptation can grow, perhaps until it becomes overpowering. Witch-Hazel couldn't think of anything much more pathetic than failing to save one's beloved because one can't avoid eating a sweet treat.

But then Witch-Hazel was a squirrel, and she had never heard the human legend of Orpheus and Eurydice. Some human legends make their way into the fairy tales told by squirrels, but that one hadn't. At least not within her family, or within her memory. Of course, Witch-Hazel wouldn't have been very impressed by Orpheus' behavior, so why would she have remembered him?

As sunset darkened to twilight and the sky turned varying shades of purple, Witch-Hazel suggested to Zwi that they stop for the night. She rather liked the tree she'd found. Some day, it would be nice to pick a tree and make a home in it once again. She missed having a home.

Zwi insisted, however, that they must push onward. "I can feel the vibrations of a fairy ring ahead, close enough we could reach it before the moon sets tonight."

"Or we could reach it before midday tomorrow morning …" Witch-Hazel proposed. She'd hung her backpack on a snag in the branch, and she didn't want to put it back on again. She was tired of the straps digging into her shoulders and the feel of its weight on her back.

"Yes," Zwi said, "but during the day, fairy rings are tended by butterflies. At night, their stewards are moths."

"And that's better?" Witch-Hazel was intrigued.

"Much better. A moth is far more likely to talk to us. Butterflies … they think they're better than everyone. At least, some of them do."

Witch-Hazel was reminded of the queen of the air realm from her vision. With those beautiful wings, it would be easy to begin putting on airs. She wondered if that related in any way to the quarrel between the four tiny royal creatures. But she had no way of knowing. At least for now. Maybe, if they were to meet with a moth soon, the moth could tell them something about the legends passed down among the keepers of the fairy rings.

Anyone who kept fairy rings must have a little magic to them, and in her mind, Witch-Hazel assumed that magical ability and the keeping of lore over the generations must tangle up together. How else could magic be managed if not by the handing down of traditions? And traditions were part of lore.

And so the bee and squirrel continued onward through dark, shadowy forest, lit only by the pearly disc of the moon, peeking through the thick branches obscuring its face.

Witch-Hazel wasn't used to traveling at night, and she kept to the forest floor, rather than risking misjudging her path and perhaps mistaking a shadow for an actual branch, high above the ground. They'd made it far enough away from the afternoon's forest fire that the air no longer stank with the spice of smoke. Instead, subtler, danker smells tickled Witch-Hazel's nose. Mushroomy smells. Wet smells. Scents that reminded her of being deep underground, splashing through rivulets beside Fish-Breath and Twiggy.

The undergrowth was all covered in droplets, slick with rainwater from the deluge earlier, that kept sinking into Witch-Hazel's fur. But this was more than that.

"There's a river up ahead," Witch-Hazel said. "I can smell it."

"Yes," Zwi agreed. "The fairy ring is beside the river."

The trees began thinning and then cleared entirely into a grassy meadow beside the rushing river. The moon had lowered behind the tree line on the other side of the river, so the water ran dark, reflecting only the dim speckling of stars from up above. But it was a clear night. The storm clouds had tired themselves out battling the fire earlier in the day, and all that was left was empty sky.

Witch-Hazel wished there was a single puffy cloud marring the stars, so she could imagine it was the cloud with the All-Being's castle on the other side and that Fish-Breath was up there looking down at her.

"I'm coming for you, Fish-Breath," Witch-Hazel whispered up at the sky, even though she knew he wasn't there. Somewhere over the edge of the horizon … just out of sight … He was somewhere, and if he could send a vision of himself to guide her, maybe he could hear her whispers too.

Witch-Hazel didn't know what powers he had access to inside the All-Being's castle. But she knew there was more magic in the world than she'd believed was real when she'd been a kit. With a gentle claw tip, she touched the air lily resting on her breast. The petal had grown brittle. The flower was drying. A terrible thought occurred to her, but Witch-Hazel refused to entertain it. Surely, the air lily would continue to work, even if it were dried instead of fresh.

"This way," Zwi buzzed, and Witch-Hazel followed her to a muddy, flat part of the riverbank.

A perfect circle of red-capped toadstools, freckled adorably with white spots, stood proudly on the bank. They looked different than the toadstools Witch-Hazel remembered from the fairy ring underground. Those had been plain and pink.

"They're different," she said. "The ones underground were pink. Does that matter?"

A voice sang out above them, clear like a bell, "Different mushrooms grow in different places. The rings can still connect to each other if the mycelia are connected under the ground."

Witch-Hazel looked up and saw a greenly tinted shadow, flapping slowly, floating and swaying in the air above. "Are you the fairy?" she asked, awestruck.

The moth drifted down and landed on one of the toadstools. She had feathery antenna and pink edges to her pale green, swallow-tailed wings. The shade of green was milkier than lime, and a touch more yellow—like lime mixed with cream to make a Key lime pie. Each quarter of her wings featured a pattern like an eye—pink around the edges; white and blue in the middle—gazing dreamily, sightlessly behind her. And her body was fat and fuzzy, white like fresh cotton. Her six legs were the same shade of pink as edged her wings.

"You're beautiful," Witch-Hazel breathed. "Exactly like a fairy should be."

Zwi landed on the red cap of the toadstool closest to the one the moth had landed on. Even without her wings, the moth was easily three times the honeybee's size. Though, from wing tip to wing tip, the vision in green was only a third the height of a squirrel.

The two insects bowed to each other, crossing their forelegs and lowering their antennae. Then the moth turned to Witch-Hazel and said in her lovely, flute-like voice, "I am a Luna moth, nothing more. But your flattery will serve you well if you ever meet with my daytime sisters, the tiger swallowtails."

The Luna moth was beautiful, but suddenly, Witch-Hazel was filled with regret that they hadn't come during the day. She had always wanted to see a tiger swallowtail up close. Their yellow and black wings, with aesthetic touches of blue and pink, were the color of dreams brought to life.

No matter. They had not come here for the simple pleasure of gazing at butterfly wings.

"We came at night specifically," Zwi buzzed. "We have a query."

"Yes, questions," Witch-Hazel agreed. "So many questions …" She wanted to ask about her vision and the Luna moth's own history, not to mention the strange dichotomy between daytime and nighttime keepers of the fairy rings, but Zwi shot her a look with her obsidian eyes that silenced her. She would let the bee take the lead; Zwi knew more about these fairies and their toadstools than her. Witch-Hazel hadn't even known fairies existed until earlier that day.

"We're seeking …" Zwi paused, antennae splaying to the sides of her head in an obsequious way. "… a vine that reaches high into the sky."

"A vine?" the Luna moth repeated. Her eyes clouded. "There are many vines."

"This one ..." Zwi lowered her head, splaying her antennae even farther to the sides. "... reaches all the way up to the All-Being's castle."

The Luna moth laughed, a sound like bells ringing or stars singing, so beautiful that Witch-Hazel was entranced. The squirrel had watched butterflies and moths float on invisible currents in the air when she was a kit, and she'd often wished to meet one. But they never flew low enough for her to see them closely, and they never answered her when she called to them.

Why would a creature of such beauty waste time on a silly squirrel kit who couldn't even keep track of acorns she buried?

Yet, here was a Luna moth, speaking to her, acknowledging her, and laughing with such a beautiful voice.

"If such a vine exists," the moth said, "and if we know of it, don't you think it would be our most closely guarded secret? Don't you think my sisters would cast me out of our society for revealing it to any bee and squirrel who happened along their way to ask about it?"

"Possibly," Zwi conceded, raising her head a little and twitching her antennae. "But what good, I ask, is the secret doing you?"

The moth ran a taloned hand along one of her feathered antennae but didn't answer.

Zwi pressed harder: "What use is a highway to the kingdoms of heaven if it's kept secret, hidden away from all who might use it?"

The moth's pink legs shuffled on the toadstool's red cap. She was nervous. Something was bothering her. Witch-Hazel wondered what it was, and if there was any way to use it to their advantage.

"You have a secret of your own," Witch-Hazel hazarded.

The Luna moth turned away, hiding her face from view. Though, Witch-Hazel couldn't read the emotions on her inscrutable insectile face anyway. The moth's true face was no more readable to a squirrel, unversed in moth expressions, than the four eyes on those lime green wings, staring with a frozen expression, coy and mysterious, but fundamentally meaningless, since they were only decorations.

But Witch-Hazel could read meaning into the Luna moth's pregnant silence. "Let us help you with your secret," she urged. "Whatever it is, if we can help, you can take that as payment for telling us how to get to the vine."

Many moments passed on the dark shore beside the river reflecting the stars. Then the Luna moth said, "Alright, I'll show you my secret."

6

THE LUNA MOTH took flight, lifting off from the red cap of the toadstool. Zwi and Witch-Hazel followed as she fluttered away from the bank of the river, back across the clearing, and into a sweetly scented shrub. In the darkness, Witch-Hazel had trouble telling the color of the flowers on the shrub, but she thought they might be purple.

The Luna moth alit on a slender branch and tilted up one of the leaves hanging above her until Witch-Hazel could see clusters of miniscu le brown spheres clinging to its underside. They were as small as the heads of pins, but they had a dusty, dirty look like truffles freshly dug from the ground.

Zwi landed lower down on the branch, giving a respectful distance to the moth.

The moth pointed with a magenta talon at the spheres and said, "These are my eggs."

Witch-Hazel wasn't sure why that qualified as a secret. Then she noticed, among the brown spheres, one of them shimmered and changed color, growing translucent and pale yellow, luminous as a pearl freshly taken from an oyster shell. Then the color shifted back to dusty brown again, and the egg looked just like all the others.

At first, Witch-Hazel thought she'd imagined the change, but as she kept watching, it happened again. And again.

"You see it?" the moth asked.

"Yes," Zwi said, answering for both of them.

"I told you a simplified version of the truth before. Those of us in the Sisterhood of the Fairy Rings aren't actually true Luna moths, nor true tiger swallowtails." As she spoke, the Luna moth's feathery antennae pointed together toward the egg that kept changing color, showing the direction of her attention. "We're a were-hybrid of each, and each individual's nature is determined by when the egg they hatch from is first laid. Those laid at night become moths; those laid during the harsh brightness of day become butterflies."

"You laid this one at the moment of dawn," Witch-Hazel said in soft, breathless words.

"Yes, I began laying too late, and had more eggs to lay than I knew." The Luna moth's forelegs crossed demurely, possibly in a sign of shame.

Though Witch-Hazel could see nothing shameful about such a beautiful egg. "What will it hatch into?"

"I don't know," the Luna moth said. "Eggs like this one are destroyed. Usually." Now she clearly looked ashamed. "But I can't bear to destroy it. The policy always made sense in the abstract ... but now that it's my own egg, and I've seen it ... It makes me wonder what we've actually been destroying."

"What would you like us to do to help?" Zwi asked.

"Take the egg with us, of course," Witch-Hazel said. "To the All-Being. Right?"

The Luna moth folded her wings behind her, and she lifted one of her forelegs from the branch. "It will hatch soon," she said. "You'll need to care for the caterpillar, and if your journey is long, guard her cocoon. Or chrysalis, I suppose. But yes, only the All-Being knows why our eggs laid at dawn or twilight turn out this way." She paused, lowering her raised foreleg several times in a restless kick. "Only the All-Being knows why our sisterhood is the way we are at all. And I must stay here, sworn to my circle, but my daughter deserves better than destruction—never hatching—for the blameless crime of having been touched by the All-Being's powers in a way we don't understand."

Witch-Hazel slipped her backpack off her shoulders, opened it, and held the bag forward, gaping open. "If you place the dawn-touched egg on its own leaf, I can keep it safe in here."

Zwi said nothing, but Witch-Hazel sensed uncertainty in her posture. Regardless, she kept holding her backpack out while the Luna moth carefully plucked the single tiny egg from the cluster.

The moth placed her egg—yellow and pearly—on an oval leaf all its own, and then rolled the leaf into the shape of a cornucopia around it. She held the green horn in her taloned hands, gazing at the egg ensconced inside long enough to see it change colors several times, before carefully placing the leafy cradle in Witch-Hazel's open backpack. It rested lightly on the bed of air lilies.

Witch-Hazel closed the backpack as carefully as she could and then slipped it back onto her shoulders.

"I suppose I'll never know if you follow through on your promise to take her to the All-Being …" the Luna moth said sadly. "Or even if she hatches, or what she'll be when she hatches. Will she be a green caterpillar like I was? Or a striped caterpillar like my daytime sisters? Or something in between? Something entirely new and different? I don't know …"

Witch-Hazel felt the urge to promise that they'd return with answers; they'd return and tell her the story of what happened. But she flattened her ears and bit her tongue. She didn't want to bind herself and Zwi with promises they might not be able to keep. Instead she said, "We'll care for her the best that we can."

Zwi bowed to the Luna moth and said, "We are honored by your trust in us. I spent several cycles in the nursery of my hive, caring for the larvae and pupae there before being sent out into the fields, becoming a harvester and scout. I will care for your offspring as if she were one of my queen's own, a very sister to myself."

The Luna moth fluttered her wings in acknowledgement and said, "I will speak to the mycelium network for you, locate the address of the vine you seek, and teach you the dance to teleport through the fairy rings to the one closest."

Before either Zwi or Witch-Hazel could respond, the Luna moth lifted off from her branch in the sweetly scented bush, took flight, and began fluttering her way across the dark clearing, back toward the river bank. Zwi flew after her.

Witch-Hazel followed the two flying insects, keenly aware of how her every movement bumped and jostled the knapsack on her back. She believed the egg would be safe, but it would be horrible if her movements damaged it. Or worse, if she somehow managed to fall and tumble, letting her backpack get squished and causing the egg to be crushed. She didn't usually fall—especially running across flat ground as she was now—but she felt the need to be particularly careful. She imagined that feeling wouldn't pass until the egg had hatched ... and even then, the feeling might only mutate to match the fetal fairy's new form.

Witch-Hazel hadn't meant to become a surrogate mother, and she wasn't sure she liked the feelings that came along with the new responsibility.

By the time the squirrel arrived at the damp dirt where the fairy ring grew, both the moth and bee were flitting through the air above the circle of toadstools in complicated patterns, dancing and twirling around each other, tracing lines of glowing light that chased them like they were shooting stars.

Witch-Hazel sat beside the river, trailing her paw in the cool flowing water, just to feel it stream between her paw pads, and watched the dizzying fireworks of the moth and bee's dance.

The trails of light spiked into stars and then smoothed into spirals, dazzling Witch-Hazel's eyes. Finally, the pattern settled into a single clear shape, like a corkscrew that narrowed as it spiraled up from the fairy ring toward the sky.

The Luna moth flew away from the ring, and then she sang in her flute-like voice, "Enter the circle now."

Witch-Hazel pulled her paw out of the river water, shook off the droplets that clung to her fur, and then hopped lightly over the closest toadstools into the glowing light. Instantly, the world around her transformed.

7

DAWN TOUCHED THE SKY, as pink and bleeding as a broken heart, where Witch-Hazel arrived. She didn't know if the sun had begun to rise already, without her noticing since she'd been too distracted by the moth and bee's luminescent dance, or if the fairy ring had teleported them far enough to the East to bring daybreak sooner.

Either way, the dawn light showed her an entirely different forest. The trees had white bark, mottled with dark patches, and sea green lichen hung from their boughs like ancient beards. An alder forest. Prickly bushes filled the undergrowth, thick with bright orange berries that glistened like edible gemstones. They smelled sour as well as sweet, and Witch-Hazel didn't think she'd like eating them. "Salmonberries …" she muttered. Her mother had told her about them. "I think my mother grew up in a forest like this one, before she traveled to the oak grove where I was born."

Witch-Hazel looked around and realized she'd been speaking to herself. Zwi had flown far too high to hear her. And with a thumping of her heart, Witch-Hazel knew why: if she got high enough, she might be able to see the vine path to the All-Being's castle in the distance. She hoped it wouldn't be too far away.

Scurrying like only a squirrel can, Witch-Hazel rattled her way up the trunk of the nearest alder, high into its canopy of branches, and finally high enough to see out over the ocean of treetops.

There it was, towards the sunrise, a single line that cut across the sky, improbably rising all the way until it disappeared into the softening eggshell blue of morning. Witch-Hazel touched the dried air lily, resting near her throat. She wished she could teleport all the way to the vine, all the way to the top of it, where she'd need the air lily's grace to survive.

But no, they were still several day's travel away.

Zwi flew back out of the out-of-reach parts of the sky and landed beside Witch-Hazel on the bowed branch she'd picked. "We should destroy the egg," she buzzed.

"What?" Witch-Hazel exclaimed, grabbing tightly onto her backpack's straps. "After the whole speech you gave? About treating the egg as one of your queen's own?"

"My queen delegates the job of destroying malformed or otherwise unnecessary eggs to the young workers serving their cycles in the nursery. I destroyed many eggs during my time there, saving the hive from wasting precious resources on extra mouths to feed at times when we didn't need them."

To a mammal like Witch-Hazel, this sounded bar-baric. But then, squirrels give birth to litters of two to eight. Not one to two thousand per day. "Regardless," she argued, "we promised to care for this egg. Aren't you worried about upsetting the Luna moth who sent us here?"

Zwi lowered her antennae in a very serious expression. "I'm more worried about upsetting the entire sisterhood of keepers of the fairy rings. If they found out what we're doing, harboring an egg they want destroyed, I might never be allowed to travel by fairy ring again."

"That would be a big cost," Witch-Hazel acknowl-edged. She'd never been able to travel by fairy ring before joining up with Zwi, and she never would be able to travel by them alone ... but she was still keenly aware of their worth. If the journey to the vine looked to be several days of hard travel now, it could have easily been weeks or months—perhaps years?—without the fairy rings to bring them closer. "However, we know this fairy ring is the one closest to the vine. So, we shouldn't encounter any more of the sisterhood of fairies on our way. How would they ever know?"

"I don't know ..." Zwi admitted. "But it seems wrong."

"Destroying the egg seems wrong to me," Witch-Hazel said. "We both come from backgrounds that set us up to see this egg in a certain way, but neither of us is part of the egg's own culture. And the only voice we've heard weigh in from that culture is the Luna moth, the egg's mother. I think we should respect her wishes."

Zwi hesitated, but eventually said, "I am worried about what it will hatch into, but ..." She glanced up at Witch-Hazel. The squirrel was so much larger than her. A literal giant who could smash the bee under paw or eat her in a single bite. A painful bite, given Zwi's stinger. But a bite no less. "I will respect the Luna moth's wishes."

"The *mother's* wishes," Witch-Hazel insisted, wary of a loophole where Zwi was secretly referring to the *other* Luna moths. The ones who would want the egg destroyed.

"Yes, the egg-layer's wishes," Zwi agreed.

Witch-Hazel felt like a bit of a bully, like she'd only gotten her way because she was bigger and Zwi couldn't overrule her. She would have to watch the egg closely and protect it.

Poor thing, it had enemies everywhere.

Since Witch-Hazel and Zwi had traveled all night long, they slept through the morning, catching up on the rest they'd missed. Witch-Hazel made sure to move her knapsack from her back to her front, so she could clutch the bag close, keeping it closed with the egg safely tucked inside.

Zwi would have trouble interfering with the precious sphere without waking her. Nonetheless, Witch-Hazel had trouble sleeping, plagued by dreams where Zwi crept under the flap closing the bag and speared the egg with her stinger, or where they returned to the fairy ring and found themselves trapped, teleporting from one ring to the next, always surrounded by the bright trails of Zwi's dancing, and never able to escape.

In other dreams, Witch-Hazel returned to the passages under the earth, and she felt both strangely satisfied to be there—at rest finally—and deeply troubled, like she was forgetting something important. Something round, and something long ...

By midday, when the sun streamed down directly from overhead, unfiltered by leaves since they'd stayed on the highest branch where Witch-Hazel could see the vine stretching into the sky in the distance, both the bee and squirrel groggily decided to give up on sleep for the day.

Witch-Hazel didn't know what had troubled Zwi's sleep. Perhaps nightmares about the other butterflies coming for her, finding the egg, and condemning her.

Witch-Hazel didn't ask.

The day's travel went smoothly, leaping from one alder to the next. For her lunch, Witch-Hazel choked down some of the distasteful, overly bitter and sour, salmonberries. But by dinner, she found that she could hold out for sweet, sweet huckleberries if she watched closely for their bushes and sniffed for their gentle scent on the wind.

Salmonberries were everywhere; huckleberries were treasures to be sought out.

Whenever they stopped, Witch-Hazel checked on the egg, a doting surrogate mother. Over the course of the day, its membranous shell seemed to soften, growing more and more translucent, whether it was dusty brown or pearly yellow.

When they stopped for the night, high in another alder tree, Witch-Hazel thought she could make out the curves of caterpillar curled inside, and excited, she called Zwi over to see.

The bee was not impressed, and once again, Witch-Hazel made a point of sleeping curled around her knapsack, guarding the precious egg. Every few hours, she woke enough to peek inside, and finally, a little before dawn, she was rewarded by seeing movement inside the egg. It had grown too translucent to tell the difference between its yellow and brown forms, and as Witch-Hazel watched raptly, the caterpillar inside chewed its way out.

Witch-Hazel saw its face first, emerging from the hole it chewed. Its face was round, brown, and strange, mostly two huge eyes with six grabby little hands right beneath it. Somehow, both adorable and bizarre.

When it crawled out, the caterpillar was nothing more than a tiny worm, covered in bristly spikes, arranged regularly over its tiny, squirmy body.

The caterpillar, still ensconced inside the rolled up leaf, immediately went to work at eating the rest of the eggshell it had so recently inhabited. As soon as the shell was gone, it started munching on the leaf around it, grabbing onto the leaf's edge with little hands and industriously chewing until the smooth edge turned ragged.

In the dim pre-dawn light, Witch-Hazel wasn't sure about the caterpillar's color, but it seemed a pale green to her, perhaps like its mother. By the time the sun had fully risen though, it had darkened to black. But then, it had also plumped up significantly from eating half of the leaf, so Witch-Hazel wasn't sure if the change in color was indicative of anything more than the change in the light and the caterpillar's rapid growth.

"We have a new mouth to feed," Zwi observed drily.

"Should we name her?" Witch-Hazel asked. "She doesn't have a mother here to name her."

"I don't know," Zwi said, somehow even more drily. "It seems to me that she does. But by all means, go ahead and name the abomination that will cause the sisterhood of the fairy rings to turn their backs on me."

Witch-Hazel stared steadily at Zwi until she lowered her antennae in a sign of submission. "It will be easier if we have something to call her by. Abomination That Will Cause The Sisterhood Of The Fairy Rings To Turn Their Backs is a little long."

In spite of herself, the bee's antennae wiggled in mirth. "Fair point. What do you suggest?"

Witch-Hazel considered the name Hope, because she hoped that rescuing the caterpillar would turn out well.

Or Faith, because she had faith that it would. But … she settled on something better: "Let's call her Mercy."

Zwi buzzed irritably. "I see what you're doing, and it will make no difference in my behavior. I won't harm the caterpillar, because you've convinced me not to. Not because you came up with a clever name to give her."

Witch-Hazel grinned. "Then you admit it's clever. And pretty, right?"

Zwi didn't answer. Instead, she took flight, and circling high above the squirrel and her new caterpillar babe, silhouetted by the pale yellow dawn sky, she said, "We have far to travel today …"

"Yes, of course. I'll be ready soon."

Quickly, Witch-Hazel pulled the last handful of clover stalks and roots from her backpack, and then she shouldered the bag onto her back. She settled Mercy on one of the shoulder straps, snatched a few alder leaves from the branch they were resting on, and tucked them under the strap where the caterpillar could reach them. "Those will make a good meal for you," she cooed at the spiky little worm. "Now hold on tight."

Fortunately, in addition to the six grabby hands at her front end, Mercy had grippy little legs in pairs running down the length of the rest of her body, and she clung onto the backpack's strap handily.

Witch-Hazel stuffed her handful of clover roots and stalks in her mouth, and then she began the daylong process of jumping from one tree to the next, bouncing along the branches, skittering along trunks to get from one good branch to the next.

The vine in the distance grew easier to see, a thicker line cutting across the sky. And Witch-Hazel grew more adept at locating huckleberry bushes, so stopping for meals didn't take as long. Also, the huckleberry bushes seemed to be growing more common, and their berries tasted even sweeter.

The trees too were changing. Their white bark brighter; their green leaves more different shades of green than was usual on a single tree, a veritable rainbow of emerald, lime, peridot, mint, moss, seafoam, and char-treuse.

"These aren't normal alder trees," Witch-Hazel whispered to herself, or maybe to the caterpillar on her shoulder. Zwi was too far ahead to hear her, as far as she knew.

Yet, the bee zoomed back through the dazzling water-fall of green leaves and said, "This forest is old. Trees like this don't grow now."

"The trees don't seem especially old ..." Witch-Hazel could tell the age of trees, and these seemed no older than the oaks in the copse where she'd grown. Perhaps, younger even.

Knowing trees like they're friends is part of being a squirrel.

"Not the trees," Zwi said. "The forest. The trees themselves are … ageless. It's like we're in a part of the world that time has forgotten."

Witch-Hazel picked a new handful of leaves to feed Mercy. The pudgy caterpillar seemed to eat constantly, and she'd already doubled in size from a skinny, prickly, squiggle of a worm to a plump, dimpled one with gorgeous black, yellow, and green stripes—thus, she must be a tiger swallowtail like her mother's daytime sisters after all.

8

Witch-Hazel had to resupply Mercy with leaves as fast as she ate them, or else the hungry, indiscriminate child tried to nibble on the squirrel's braided air lily necklace. And that wouldn't do.

"I need that flower," Witch-Hazel scolded in a cooing, baby voice. "Without it, I can't save my friend, or take you where your mother asked me to take you."

Zwi overheard the squirrel admonishing the caterpillar babe and flew back to say, "If all you say to her is a few words here and there about what she can and can't do, that grub will learn nothing. You must sing to her."

"Sing to her?" Witch-Hazel asked, continuing to climb from branch to branch. It was nice to have Zwi paying attention to her again. Usually, they chatted as they traveled, at least a little. But today, the bee had kept her distance, seemingly too angry about the caterpillar's presence to even acknowledge her.

"Yes, sing to her of the history of … well, not her people. But yours. Stories. Tales. Anything that will teach her." Zwi paused in her flight, hovering near Witch-Hazel's shoulder.

The squirrel stopped on the branch she'd been traveling along to look at the bee.

"When I served my cycles in the nursery," Zwi said, "we sang to the eggs, larvae, and pupae. All day, we sang."

"Would you sing to her?" Witch-Hazel asked.

Zwi flitted away into the blue sky, and for a moment, Witch-Hazel wondered whether the bee had decided to abandon them entirely, return to her solo quest and forget about the quest they shared.

But Zwi returned, buzzing angrily, and said, "Only because I don't want a fool for a traveling companion, and this caterpillar will grow into a fool fast without my help."

"Mercy does seem to be growing fast," Witch-Hazel agreed, pointedly ignoring the bee's barbed commentary regarding her parenting abilities.

But then squirrels aren't used to raising caterpillars. Witch-Hazel had helped her littermates with their own litters several times before, and if Mercy were a squirrel, the babe would be doing just fine. She also wouldn't be growing up nearly so fast.

For the rest of the day, Zwi flew along beside Witch-Hazel, companionably singing epic tales of hive after hive, queen after queen, and one blessed tree after another, each succeeding the last when a young queen decided to forge out on her own and establish a new hive.

Zwi's people had a beautiful history, and although Witch-Hazel couldn't understand all of it, she loved listening to the cadences and rhythms, the sing-song quality of a bee singing lullabies to a child.

As they got closer to the vine, they were able to see how it stretched farther into the sky and began to be able to make out the puffy white cloud, far, far above the world.

Witch-Hazel's heart quickened at the sight. She could almost feel Fish-Breath's presence up there, on the other side of that cloud, inside a golden castle she couldn't quite see.

When sunset spilled across the sky like strawberry lemonade, the cloud at the top of the vine turned gold around the edges and bubblegum pink in the middle.

At the moment of sundown, without discussing what they were doing, Witch-Hazel stopped where she was, at the corner between branch and trunk in an alder tree, and Zwi landed on her shoulder, opposite the caterpillar.

They both watched Mercy carefully, and as the light changed, her stripes vanished, blushing green until her whole pudgy body was green, except for regular pink dimples.

A Luna moth caterpillar. Like her mother. Except, all day long, she'd been a tiger swallowtail, like the daytime sisters.

"If she's going to change form every day at dawn and sunset," Zwi said, "we'll have to make sure that any moths or butterflies we meet along the way only see her either at night or during the day. Not both."

"She can sleep in my backpack at night," Witch-Hazel said. Though, she couldn't help worrying that Mercy would eat her stash of extra air lilies, if she were left alone for hours, curled up in their tempting leaves and petals. Even Witch-Hazel wanted to eat them, and she wasn't driven by a caterpillar's hunger.

"Yes," Zwi agreed. "That would be best. Then we can hide her shifting nature from everyone, not just moths and butterflies. That will be safer."

Safer for Mercy, perhaps. But not the air lilies.

Before they slept that night, Witch-Hazel braided the rest of the air lilies into a garland that could be easily removed from her backpack and draped over her shoulders when Mercy needed to hide inside the bag. Then she filled the backpack with a full night's worth of alder and huckleberry leaves, assuming the caterpillar would continue eating through much of the night. She threw in a few fern fiddleheads for variety, uncertain of whether Mercy would like them.

Zwi insisted that their hungry ward begin practicing sleeping inside the backpack, so she would already be trained to hide there if the need arose. Witch-Hazel agreed—partly, she thought Zwi was right; partly, she thought Mercy would be safer in the backpack from Zwi herself.

For three more days, they continued their travels in much the same way. Zwi sang to a striped caterpillar, perched on Witch-Hazel's shoulder and busy munching on leaves, all day long, from the time they began travelling until the sun went down. When Zwi tired of singing, Witch-Hazel took a turn, singing whatever nut-gathering chanties she could recall.

As soon as twilight came though, Witch-Hazel placed the pudgy green caterpillar safely inside her backpack, where the babe continued eating piles of leaves as the squirrel and bee traveled under the stars, until they were too tired to go on and found a cozy crook between branches in the crown of an alder where they could stop for the night.

The forest continued to change around them as they traveled, and the vine continued to thicken in the distance. It was clearly much wider around than Witch-Hazel had originally guessed. She had assumed it would be as thick around as a wide tree, but she began to suspect the base of the vine's trunk was closer to the width of the entire lake where she'd hidden from the forest fire and found the air lilies, meaning they were also farther away from it than she'd first realized.

But a squirrel and a bee, laden only by a light back-pack, can travel fast, especially in a forest overflowing with delicious nuts and berries. The farther they went, the more types of berries Witch-Hazel found—blackberries, blue-berries, raspberries, loganberries, gooseberries ... a whole rainbow of delectable fruits. Types of berries she'd never seen before, and types she was almost certain shouldn't grow in the same climate as each other, nor ripen at the same time.

Witch-Hazel's belly was always full, yet her tongue kept craving more of the sweet, flavorful juices. She wished she were as hungry as Mercy, who never stopped eating.

By the end of the fourth day since they'd teleported through the fairy ring, the vine had become a green swath of jungle, smeared across the blue sky. Witch-Hazel could no longer see the puffy cloud at the top of the vine, because the towering highway of green blocked its view, seemingly filling a quarter of the dimming sky.

The sun hadn't set yet, but Witch-Hazel stopped on a branch, pulled her backpack off, and nudged Mercy from the strap she clung to, guiding her bunchy-backed crawling with a gentle paw, until she'd crawled into the opening of the backpack. Witch-Hazel pulled out the garland of air lilies, arranged them around her shoulders, and then stuffed several handfuls of tasty leaves into the backpack before replacing it carefully on her shoulders, straps beneath the delicate garland.

Zwi hovered nearby, rotating her antennae quizzically.

"Just being cautious," Witch-Hazel said. "I feel … we're close." She was excited about reaching the vine, touching it with her claws, and finding out what it felt like to climb. Would the green flesh be soft and giving like a new squash vine that grows anew every summer? Or hard and woody like the bark of a tree that's stood proudly since time immemorial?

The mere idea of sinking her claws into it and beginning to skitter upwards into the sky made her silver tail twitch and wave like a flag on a windy day.

Would it be windy in the sky?

The alder trees grew thickly here, and Witch-Hazel couldn't see very far ahead. Suddenly, she realized her view through the dappled forest canopy had become completely obscured by the folds of sea green lichen hanging on the trees like beards. The folds fell so closely together, they'd joined into one, forming a solid curtain, curving away from them in each direction.

"Well, that's exciting," Witch-Hazel said.

"Or ominous," Zwi countered. "I'm glad you put the munchy mouth away."

Witch-Hazel wasn't entirely certain if "munchy mouth" counted as an endearing pet name or merely ridicule for Mercy. But she agreed it was safer to have Mercy hidden before passing through the curtain of lichen.

Witch-Hazel approached the lichen beards and gingerly touched the rough yet lacy substance with an outstretched paw. Neither plant nor fungus, the lichen was both. A living being that straddled two forms of existence, like the caterpillar hidden and munching away inside her backpack.

Witch-Hazel pushed aside the lichen beard in front of her and stepped along the canopy branch she'd been traveling across, but each step she took between the hanging beards just brought her up against more beards to push aside. Worse, the beards hung from the branches, and Witch-Hazel could no longer find steady footing among the piles of lichen. With each footstep, she had to carefully judge where the actual branch was hidden beneath the frothy green—a green so pale that it looked more like the skeleton of a shade of green that had died.

When Witch-Hazel guessed wrong about which way the branches turned beneath the lichen, her footing wobbled, threatening to tear the lichen free and send her tumbling.

Better to climb down to the ground of her own accord than to fall there against her wishes. "I'm climbing down," she said, unable to see where Zwi had flown to between the hanging beards.

With her feet back on the ground, Witch-Hazel felt steadier, and she wove her way relatively quickly between the beards that dripped all the way down to brush against the forest floor.

"Zwi?" Witch-Hazel called out. "Do you hear me? I've climbed down to the ground." The thickness of the lichen dampened the sound of her voice. It wouldn't carry far here, and she had little hope that Zwi had heard her. She couldn't hear Zwi's buzzing anywhere. Only the muffled sound of her own feet treading over the loamy ground and the frightened racing of her heart.

Was this curtain of lichen a barrier? Meant to keep intruders out? Perhaps, designed to discourage anyone from questing to the All-Being's castle in the clouds …

9

THE SUN HAD BEEN close to setting before Witch-Hazel and Zwi entered the curtain of lichen, and it must have been all the way down by now because all the light was gone. There should have been moonlight and starlight from above, but the lichen beards blotted any light from them out. Too thick. So, Witch-Hazel found herself pressing forward, holding her paws in front of her to feel her away.

Lichen brushed against her, and she tried to keep it out of her face, but there was too much. She kept walking right into the ephemeral curtains, and it reminded her of the unpleasant feeling of walking into an overly ambitious spider's web, getting a mouthful of icky, sticky silk. Her fur would be covered with bits of broken off lichen before this was over. And no matter how much she spat out of her mouth, she was surely going to end up swallowing some of the bitter, musty stuff.

Disgruntled, Witch-Hazel's ears flattened, and her tail whipped frenetically behind her. She held onto the image of Fish-Breath's cheerful face to keep her going, blindly feeling her way through the dark.

She wished she still had one of the candle crystals that she'd used to light her way through the subterranean caverns and passageways of her last journey. The spherical rocks had felt so solid and grounding in her paw, and their flickering blue light had made everything look magical.

Her memory of the light was so strong, and her desire for it so powerful, Witch-Hazel began to see dappled blue light dancing before her eyes, as if she really did clutch a candle crystal in her paw. Perhaps her eyes were playing tricks on her? She hadn't been anywhere this dark since emerging from the underground labyrinth, and the light she saw might be nothing more than an artifact of her own eyes trying to interpret the darkness.

Then the flickering lights began to draw lines and squiggles in the air between the folds of lichen, reminiscent of the glowing spell Zwi and the Luna moth had cast to activate the magic of the fairy ring.

Witch-Hazel didn't think she could be imagining such complicated, arcane figures. Something real was behind those blue bits of light.

"Zwi?" Witch-Hazel asked again, wishing for the comfort of her friend's voice. Yet she expected no response. Sound didn't travel far enough here.

Witch-Hazel narrowed her eyes, peering as closely as she could at the fleeting sparks of light. She thought they might be coming from fireflies, or maybe something more mythical—will-o'-the-wisps that would lead her astray if she followed them. But they didn't seem to be trying to guide her, either toward her goal or away from it. They weren't dancing for her—just dancing.

But she appreciated how their growing light had begun to illuminate the cascading folds of lichen. The forest here was mystically beautiful.

Finally, Witch-Hazel stepped past a particularly broad lichen beard, and the view cleared in front of her. Her heart nearly stopped at the sight of a wide, dark clearing, sparkling with the dancing lights, and only a few feet in front of her, a white mare, glowing softly like the moon, with one foreleg held daintily crooked, and her head lowered. A horn sprouted from her brow, spiraling like a seashell and as richly luminous as mother of pearl—it was more than silver, more than rainbow; more like both blended together.

Zwi had perched at the tip of the unicorn's horn, and Witch-Hazel's heart clenched at the sight. She felt drawn to the unicorn, like she would trade the air lilies draped over her shoulders, the were-caterpillar happily munching inside of her backpack, and even her own silver tail if it meant she too could touch that glowing horn.

The unicorn raised her head and whinnied, "Welcome, traveler. You've come a long way."

At the sound of the unicorn's voice, Witch-Hazel let out a breath she hadn't realized she was holding. The unicorn's beauty was literally breathtaking.

But even now that Witch-Hazel was breathing again, no words came to her. She could find no words inside herself, anywhere, to say to this magnificent creature whose color shifted from the brightness of snow in the morning to the softness of dandelion down as swiftly as dappled light danced through a forest when wind rustled the leaves.

"Your friend tells me that you wish to travel up the beanstalk to the All-Being's realm," said the unicorn. Her voice danced like songbird's, but with a deeper resonance, warm and soothing. "And I see you've brought the air lilies you'll need. Very clever!"

Witch-Hazel's ears burned pink beneath her fur. The unicorn had praised her! Yet, deep inside, she heard an echo of the last individual who had called her clever—the sorcerous snake who had lured her down into the labyrinth beneath the earth, tried to steal the Celestial Treasures she'd gathered, and wounded Fish-Breath so badly that the only way to save him had been to send him with the Celestial Treasures into the sky, to the All-Being's breast.

But this unicorn was nothing like the snake sorcerer, leader of an undead army. Accepting the praise—letting it inside herself to warm her heart—could do no harm.

"Th-thank you, m'lady." Witch-Hazel stumbled over the words, feeling her tongue was too clumsy to speak to such a graceful being.

The unicorn laughed like water in a brook babbling over the smooth stones beneath, worn round over centuries. Both ancient as time and fresh as running water all at once. "So formal! Please, call me Gloaming, and Zwi tells me that you are Witch-Hazel?"

The squirrel nodded, mutely.

"I know you're in a hurry to begin climbing the beanstalk, but it looks like you've been traveling all day?"

Witch-Hazel nodded again.

"Well, you certainly can't begin the next leg of your journey without rest first." Gloaming pawed at the ground with the hoof she'd been holding up, and she tilted her head, seemingly lost in thought, or maybe dreams. She looked like a creature who belonged in dreams, not standing here before them, as real as moonlight, and also as elusive. "You must stay here tonight, under my protection, of course. And if you'll be here in the morning anyway, then you simply must attend the fox wedding."

Witch-Hazel's eyes widened. "Fox … wedding?" She'd thought those were myths. Although, she supposed that foxes must have relationships, regardless of the silly stories squirrels make up about them. Why not weddings? Still, it seemed very coincidental. Almost as if the universe had read her mind and delivered exactly the fairy story she'd been thinking about mere days ago.

And also, kind of threatening.

What business would a squirrel have at a fox wedding? Appetizer? Hors d'oeuvre? The whole point of fox weddings was that they kept foxes busy, so squirrels could easily avoid them.

"Well, fox and rabbit," Gloaming corrected herself. "The groom is a rabbit, but the bride is a fox. She could use another bridesmaid."

Witch-Hazel had so many questions, but also, her eyes were so heavy. She hadn't realized how tired she was, until the unicorn suggested she and Zwi needed to rest.

Gloaming began trotting away, and Witch-Hazel found herself following the white vision of grace without being told or asked. The unicorn led her through a grove of trees. Witch-Hazel couldn't make out what kinds most of them were in the dark, lit only by the dim dancing of the blue lights—either fireflies or will-o'-the-wisps. Perhaps both. Many of the trees seemed to be laden with fruit.

Gloaming led the tired squirrel to a weeping willow tree, another curtain of cascading greens that reminded her of the lichen beards. Everything here seemed to be hidden behind folds of green, parting only when you got close enough to push them aside. It made Witch-Hazel jumpy, uncertain as to whether something might be waiting, just out of sight, ready to attack. Perhaps a fox from tomorrow's wedding party.

Yet, she felt that she should be at ease. She had made it to the grove of trees surrounding the base of the beanstalk, and she and Zwi had been greeted by an honest to goodness unicorn who had promised them protection.

How much safer could they be than in a unicorn's glen?

The unicorn was clearly the keeper of the beanstalk, and she had kept it here for all these years, as every other connection between the land and sky had crumbled. She must have powerful magic. And now Witch-Hazel and Zwi were under the protection of her powerful magic too, for as long as they rested here before beginning the next leg of their journey.

The weeping willow had a large knothole just below the point where its trunk split into two wide branches. Gloaming invited Witch-Hazel and Zwi to make themselves at home there, and it truly was the perfect size and shape for a squirrel's nest. It was even stuffed with dried leaves and bits of twigs already. Witch-Hazel hadn't felt so much at home since … well, since her journey had begun, and she'd left the oak copse where her family still lived.

"Doesn't it seem strange," Zwi buzzed, "that you were talking about fox weddings only days ago, and now we've been invited to one?"

Witch-Hazel waved the bee's concerns away, saying they'd discuss it in the morning. She was too tired now to do anything more than stuff a few handfuls of fresh willow leaves in the backpack for Mercy, and then curl up in the nest of twigs and dried leaves to sleep.

When dawn came, waking them softly with the touch of pale yellow light, Zwi's concerns had melted away like the stars at daybreak. Her night had been filled with dreams and prophecies, rich visions sent to her by the All-Being who had blessed the weeping willow tree where they'd slept. The first blessed tree she had encountered on their entire journey. She couldn't care less about fox weddings.

10

GLOAMING CAME TO Witch-Hazel and Zwi shortly after the yellow light of dawn had softened to the clear light of day.

A small red fox sat upon the unicorn's back, black feet tucked neatly beneath the curl of a fluffy, white-tipped tail. Her orange ears splayed to the sides, making her look confused and uncertain. She had a garland of tiny, white, star-like flowers draped around her neck.

Gloaming introduced the fox—today's bride-to-be named Carnelian—to the squirrel and bee, and then explained she was feeling nervous about her pending nuptials and wished to get away from the pressure of her and her groom's families for a while.

"It's too many foxes asking why I'd marry a bunny, and too many bunnies worrying about whether they should be afraid I'll eat them." Carnelian lowered her head, but kept looking up with her bright eyes at the knothole where Witch-Hazel and Zwi were perched, giving her a submissive, subservient expression. "You're not afraid of me, are you?"

Witch-Hazel was surprised to discover that she wasn't. The fox looked too sweet in her bridal flowers, too unsure of herself, and also, too much like a figure in a dream. Besides, Gloaming had promised her protection. "No," Witch-Hazel said. "I'm not."

"Would you … would you help me finish preparing for the wedding?" Carnelian asked. "And be my maid of honor? All of my sisters have refused. They don't like Harvey, my betrothed. So, they'll wear flower garlands and stand beside me during the ceremony … but they won't help."

"I'd be honored," Witch-Hazel said. Her own litter-mates had all relegated her to minor roles at their own weddings, not trusting her with any responsibility.

"Very good," Gloaming announced. "Then I shall leave you all to your breakfasts and preparations."

"Wait!" Zwi buzzed. The bee took flight from the twig she'd been using as her bed all night, flew over to the unicorn, and danced about the tip of her horn, buzzing excitedly about the visions she'd had during her dreams and the blessing from the All-Being she felt upon the willow tree.

"Well, of course the willow is blessed," Gloaming said when Zwi finally settled down. "All the trees in my grove are blessed by the All-Being."

Zwi hovered in the air, looking flabbergasted. At long last, she had fulfilled her quest, and she hadn't seen her success coming. She'd expected to have to travel so much farther and then reckon with the whims of a god.

"If you liked the visions you had while sleeping in the willow," Gloaming said, "you should try sleeping in the other trees as well. Each one has a different character."

Zwi somersaulted in the air, loop-de-looping in wild patterns. Witch-Hazel had never seen the tiny bee so overwhelmed with happiness, completely overcome by her own feelings.

"Trees to choose from!" Zwi buzzed happily before floating away, out through a gap in the willow's draping branches to find another tree to try.

Witch-Hazel could hardly blame her. Zwi had found a new home for her hive—potentially a whole grove of trees for them to choose between.

Witch-Hazel imagined she'd be similarly overcome if she'd found Fish-Breath waiting for her in this grove …

He'd make a fantastic escort to a wedding. Handsome and dapper. But also … goofy and fun. Everything had seemed better when Witch-Hazel had been traveling with him. And even though they'd only known each other for a short time, she felt his absence everywhere, a sad presence that was constantly with her. His absence made a much worse traveling companion than Fish-Breath himself.

Carnelian hopped down from Gloaming's back, and then the unicorn turned and trotted away, leaving the fox and squirrel alone together.

Witch-Hazel had doubts about coming down from her safe knothole, several feet up the trunk of the willow tree. All of her instincts screamed that squirrels don't approach foxes. But she would never have met Zwi or Fish-Breath if she'd followed those sorts of instincts, because she would never have heard the snake's song that sent her questing for the Celestial Treasures deep underground.

Besides, if she didn't distract herself with the fox's wedding, Witch-Hazel might have to think about the fact that Zwi no longer had a reason to accompany her in climbing up the beanstalk to the All-Being's castle. Witch-Hazel might well find herself climbing into the sky for days on end with only a mute, hungry caterpillar as a traveling companion. That sounded lonely and frightening.

So, instead of listening to her instincts or thinking about her future, Witch-Hazel replaced the air lilies in her backpack and stashed the bag in the back of the knothole. Then she settled Mercy on her shoulders with a long dangling twig of willow leaves for her to eat and climbed down to the ground to meet a fox.

Carnelian paraded Witch-Hazel through the grove like they were long lost best friends, introducing her to everyone else in the wedding party—fox bridesmaids and bunny groomsmen—and showing off all the decorations—garlands of flowers in every color; wreaths of cheerfully orange and red, out-of-season, autumnal leaves; and trellises made from thin branches braided into beautiful awnings and archways, culminating in a gazebo positively draped with pale, pastel colored flowers.

Witch-Hazel and Carnelian sat in a four-leaf clover patch beneath the gazebo, braiding flower garlands for each other and giggling over stories from each of their pasts, while various fox cousins of the bride brought them breakfast, snacks, and other refreshments. To Witch-Hazel's delight, every article of food was vegetarian—tiny pies and quiches, loaded with juicy berries or savory mushrooms; fresh leafy salads; and roasted, sugared nuts.

Witch-Hazel was enjoying herself too much to worry about the strangeness of foxes eating exactly what she, herself, would like to eat. And she didn't mind the foxes cooing over how cute Mercy was either. She'd been enjoying raising the caterpillar over the last few days, and it was nice to have others share in her enjoyment, instead of muttering imprecations about how the were-caterpillar would be the doom of them all.

The day raced past in a joyous parade of pageantry.

The fox bridesmaids looked beautiful with their pink flower garlands against their ruddy fur; the bunny grooms-men—especially Harvey—looked handsome in their dark purple garlands. Dark purple apparently looked good against an entire range of fur colors—brown, orange, white, gray, speckled, and splotched. The groom himself was an all white rabbit, like a giant marshmallow, and the orchids he wore, dark and royal, set off his snowy complexion perfectly.

The wedding ceremony—where all the foxes and bunnies sat in orderly rows around the gazebo—was followed by a heavenly feast and riotous dancing to music sung by a veritable orchestra of songbirds perched in the trees.

With Mercy happily settled in the pink flower garlands Witch-Hazel was wearing, the two of them joined in the dancing. All kinds of forest animals came to the party, and Witch-Hazel found herself dancing in the arms of one creature after another, passed from paw to paw as everyone merrily changed partners. Everyone dancing with everyone. Witch-Hazel danced with the marshmallow of a groom; then Carnelian, whose eyes glinted with happiness; then one vulpine bridesmaid after another. She danced with a chipmunk half her height, and badger who towered over her. At one point, she found herself in the arms of a river otter, and he looked so much like Fish-Breath—so much like the otter who had led her to the air lilies deep beneath the lake—that she gasped. But before she could speak to him, the handsome otter was gone, mixed into the crowd, and she was dancing with a red squirrel, a mirror of herself with pointier ears and fur like the flames during the forest fire.

At one point, Witch-Hazel looked up at the sky, imagining that if she could see the cloud far above them, at the top of the beanstalk, it would be like looking at Fish-Breath, connecting with him, even from an impossible distance. She couldn't make out the sky clearly enough through the tangle of flower garlands and braided trellises above the dancing throng, but she did notice a throng of dancers—a swarm of flying insects, dancing to the music, just like the mammals below. Fireflies, ladybugs, beetles, and all types of bees.

In the dimming light, she thought she spotted Zwi dancing with a dragonfly, four times her size. The bee looked happy.

Witch-Hazel felt happy too, but the dimming light reminded her that she needed leave the dance. She had to take her young, hungry ward away from the festivities before the caterpillar's striking stripes morphed into solid verdigris.

Witch-Hazel barely made it back to the knothole in the willow tree, where she'd stashed her backpack, before the sun finished setting. The day had escaped her. Yet she couldn't regret a moment of it. Being taken in as the best friend of a fox bride had been a magical experience. She and Mercy would sleep in the willow tree again, and in the morning, they could find Zwi, say their goodbyes, and begin traveling again.

But in the morning, Gloaming came to Witch-Hazel and told her a roost of monarch butterflies were on their way to the grove and would arrive by early afternoon.

"They come only twice a year, as part of their migration, and it's a sight to behold!"

Witch-Hazel could hardly turn down staying to see a sight that a unicorn thought was worth beholding. The unicorn was a sight worth seeing herself. How beautiful must the monarch migration be in order to impress her? Besides, Witch-Hazel had traveled so far, with so little rest. Another day would make little difference.

For all she knew, Fish-Breath was having the time of his life in the All-Being's castle and would prefer it if she took a few extra days to get there and rescue him. He was probably enjoying feasts and dances with the All-Being, just like she was in the unicorn's grove.

So, Witch-Hazel stayed to see the monarch butterflies, telling herself that Mercy deserved to meet a few creatures who were closer to her own kind. They picnicked with Gloaming as the orange and black butterflies flew in, fluttering like bits of stained glass come to life, so thick they filled the sky.

The butterflies sang songs and told stories of their travels, and another day passed away. And then another, for the monarch swarm took several days to entirely pass through the grove, and Witch-Hazel couldn't tear herself away from their fascinating gossip and cheerful chatter.

A few days stretched into a few more, and soon days became weeks. Witch-Hazel and Zwi fell into a routine. Every night after hiding Mercy away in the backpack, Zwi came to the willow tree and told Witch-Hazel about the dreams she'd had while napping her life away in each tree of the grove.

A tree with delectably sour green apples had shown Zwi visions of her hive growing so strong and fruitful that they would send princesses out to start hives of their own in all the neighboring apple trees. But a pear tree showed Zwi visions of a hive that stayed small, yet grew in their creativity and artistry, until their dances were celebrated by other hives far and wide.

The weeping willow's vision continued to tantalize Zwi too—it had showed her worker bee sisters constructing a hive with her that spiraled around the tree's trunk and sprouted turrets and spires like a castle. An architectural marvel.

The ecstatic bee could not choose which vision she loved best, which future she wanted for her hive. She didn't know which tree should become their new home, and so during the days, she kept napping in the trees, dreaming new visions, and at night, she tried to balance their beauties, discussing them with Witch-Hazel, who was equally unable to help her choose between them all.

And through it all, Mercy munched away at whatever leaves Witch-Hazel gave her, quietly watching and listening to everything that happened.

11

EVERYTHING COULD HAVE stayed that way forever—Zwi dithering over different trees, and Witch-Hazel distracted by the unicorn's jam-packed schedule of daily activities—as the bee and squirrel grew older and eventually died.

But caterpillars don't stay caterpillars.

And one morning, Witch-Hazel opened her backpack to find a chrysalis inside, instead of a caterpillar. At first, she didn't recognize the chrysalis, thinking it was only a strange, lumpy twig. She nearly panicked, worrying that Mercy had climbed out of the backpack during the night, looking for more leaves to eat, and had gotten lost. But recognition dawned on her, and she felt a surge of pride. She and Zwi had successfully raised a caterpillar all the way through its childhood.

The chrysalis, of course, changed shape at night, transforming into a cocoon, much more rounded and a ruddier shade of brown. If anything, being able to leave Mercy safely in the willow tree all day, hidden inside the stashed backpack, without worrying about feeding her, freed Witch-Hazel to fall even farther under the unicorn's spell. The carefree squirrel was suddenly free to dance the nights away in the unicorn's magical grove, sparing only enough thought for Mercy to check on her chrysalis in the mornings and her cocoon at night.

But chrysalises don't stay chrysalises. And cocoons break open.

Mercy emerged from her metamorphosis at the precise moment of dawn. She'd begun struggling against the confines of her cocoon in dark purple twilight before morning, but it was a strenuous process, breaking her way out, shoving her head through the cracks as they formed. And by the time she stepped, on wobbly, spindly, long legs onto the paw Witch-Hazel held out for her, the golden disc of the sun had broken over the horizon, far away, hidden by the trees of the grove. Yet somehow, her were-body knew, and her fuzzy, white, barrel-chested thorax slimmed, smoothed, and darkened to the rich yellow of butter, highlighted by elegant black stripes. Her wet wings changed from the green of wilted leaves to a complex tapestry of yellow, black, blue, and red. Though they stayed crumpled and took many minutes to dry.

Witch-Hazel marveled at the beautiful creature perched so delicately on her paw. Mercy was as light as a leaf; she groomed her new antennae—long and black— with her new talon hands, straightening them out from the mussed skew they'd begun with. Maybe she had no choice, since Witch-Hazel had been watching her emerge from the cocoon-come-chrysalis ever since awaking with an eerie feeling of portent, but Mercy stood so trustingly on the squirrel's paw. It melted Witch-Hazel's heart. Perhaps, all she had done was be there at a time when the new butterfly was vulnerable and couldn't turn her away, but it still made for an intimate, precious moment.

Witch-Hazel had protected the caterpillar for weeks, and now her heart burst with the need to protect the butterfly Mercy had become.

And that meant leaving the grove.

Today.

Before the sun set and Mercy changed forms. Because Witch-Hazel couldn't cram those delicate wings inside the tight confines of her backpack. She couldn't hide Mercy's unstable form from Gloaming. So, they had to leave.

It was like Witch-Hazel had finally woken up from a month long sleep. She looked around the grove, and she realized nothing had been real. She remembered dancing and feasting—but her dance partners had the changing quality of figures in dreams, and the food had been much simpler than it seemed at the time. Just fruit and nuts picked from the trees in the grove.

The trees were real. But ... Carnelian ... and Harvey ... and the monarch butterflies with their songs of faraway places ... None of them had been anything but shadows cast by the unicorn's magic.

All of Witch-Hazel's memories were hazy. And finally the scales had fallen from her eyes. The unicorn's magic no longer bewitched her. At least, not completely.

As Witch-Hazel trekked through the grove of fruit and nut trees—backpack on her back and Mercy perched on her shoulder, wings drying—she could still see the shadows of the braided trellises and the fancifully carved gourds and squashes from the festival yesterday. But they were insubstantial, like reflections on glass.

Carnelian came to Witch-Hazel and, after marveling at Mercy's new swallowtail wings, invited her to join the others for breakfast, gesturing at a feast-laden table. But Witch-Hazel could see right through all of it. She didn't answer the shadow being, but that only caused Carnelian to follow her. The wispy ghost of a fox pleaded, growing increasingly insistent. Her husband, the marshmallowy Harvey, bounced along beside them, also begging Witch-Hazel and Mercy to come to breakfast.

Finally, Witch-Hazel could take their keening cries no more, and she said, feeling as though she were talking to the air itself, "Yes, yes, I'll be there soon. I just want ... to find Zwi first. She needs to see Mercy's new wings too. Right away."

The shadows seemed to understand her and returned to praising the beauty of Mercy's swallowtail wings. At least, Witch-Hazel believed they were praising and flattering the beauty of the wings ... But she couldn't quite make out their words. She caught the occasional phrase— "yellow as sunlight" or "rainbow come to life"—but most of it was nothing more than a general sense of their meaning and intentions.

The young butterfly flapped her drying wings slowly, seemingly absorbing the incoherent praise from the fox- and rabbit-shadows with a critical eye, staying as silent as she'd always been during her weeks as a caterpillar.

Witch-Hazel had halfway expected—and definitely hoped—that Mercy would begin speaking once she'd taken on her adult form. But then, why bother speaking when most of the words you heard modelled for you were jumbled like this? Incoherent ramblings from shadows …

Witch-Hazel wondered what it must be like to have lived nearly one's entire life in this grove, surrounded by Gloaming's magical shadows. Did anything seem real to Mercy? Could she tell the difference between real and false? And if she couldn't, was that Witch-Hazel's fault?

The squirrel's ears burned with shame. She'd been such a fool to be taken in like this. She was supposed to be climbing the beanstalk, rescuing Fish-Breath … and instead, she'd been dancing with shadows. Literally dancing with them. She was a fool. Maybe … it hurt to think this, but she had to think it … maybe Fish-Breath was better off without her.

But then, Fish-Breath had loved foolishness. He'd savored silliness. No, he wouldn't hold this against her. He'd understand.

If she found him.

When she found him.

But she needed to find Zwi first.

The bee was dancing with an ant drone—the drones have wings, and they were both flying, or perhaps talking, since dance is a kind of language for bees—in the space above a rose bush that was positively festooned with bright red blossoms. Except, the bush, the blossoms, and the ant drone with his shimmery wings and shiny red carapace were all shadows. None of it was real, except for the bee. Dancing alone.

"Zwi, we need to talk," Witch-Hazel said.

Zwi buzzed, irritably, "Can't you see I'm in the middle of discussing the benefits of a hive expanding to multiple hives versus focusing on the improvement of a single hive? I'll find you later when we're done."

"No," Witch-Hazel barked through gritted teeth. "Come with me now."

Zwi buzzed exasperatedly, but then she politely excused herself from the shadow of an ant drone. He seemed like a very handsome shadow, and Witch-Hazel wondered whether there'd been more to Zwi's dancing with him than discussing hive civics. Could a worker bee and an ant drone be sharing a romantic fling?

In this garden, Witch-Hazel supposed, anything was possible. She'd personally watched a fox marry a rabbit, and played the part of bridesmaid in their wedding. Something that would never happen outside the glamours of a unicorn's grove.

She couldn't believe how naive she'd been.

Once the shadow of an ant drone had flown away, Zwi asked, "Now tell me what's so important."

Witch-Hazel gestured to the butterfly perched on her shoulder expressively. "Mercy emerged from her … chrysalis." She stumbled over the word, nearly calling it a cocoon by mistake. She didn't know how close the unicorn was. She didn't know if Gloaming was listening.

"Delightful," Zwi buzzed.

"Yes, but also …" Witch-Hazel glanced around furtively. She was surrounded by the shadows of rose bushes—bright colored flowers that only pretended to exist. Gloaming must be casting them, but did that mean she was awake? Or nearby? Could she keep up these glamours while she slept? Did unicorns sleep?

Witch-Hazel felt so overwhelmed and ignorant. This unicorn had gone to a lot of trouble to keep her here, creating distractions for her—perfectly tailored to her—every single day.

What would Gloaming do to stop her, once the unicorn realized she was finally set on leaving?

Witch-Hazel had fought ghost moles, zombie lizards, and a sorcerer snake.

And she'd won.

But she didn't think she'd win in a fight against a unicorn.

"What?" Zwi said. "Tell me what you're here to tell me, or let me go back to my conversation …"

"Mercy and I are leaving," Witch-Hazel said, quietly as she could. The words were little more than breath, but even breathing them felt dangerous.

"I wish you well," Zwi said. "We traveled together a long way, and I would never have found this grove—this new home for my hive—if it weren't for you. I owe you many thanks. My entire hive does."

Witch-Hazel was touched by the change in Zwi's tone. The bee sounded truly regretful that they would be parting ways. But as Witch-Hazel had feared, Zwi planned to stay here.

Witch-Hazel couldn't let her friend stay in an enchanted grove, dancing with shadows, without warning her of the danger.

"Have you … have you picked a tree?"

"Not yet. But soon I think."

"Really?" Witch-Hazel pressed.

"I've been narrowing it down," Zwi buzzed defensively.

"… have you? Truly? To which trees? Fruit trees? Nut trees? The willow?"

"Each has its advantage ..." Zwi began, and Witch-Hazel could instantly sense that the bee was trying to fall into one of their circuitous conversations, weighing the advantages and disadvantages of every future she'd been shown in her visions from the trees. It was a conversation they'd had many times, in the evenings after tucking Mercy away for the night, and they had looped through the same rhetorical paths over and over again until they'd been worn smooth, like deer trails through a forest where the underbrush has been cleared away by the regular beating of hooves.

"No, no, no!" Witch-Hazel exclaimed. "Don't you see you could keep doing this forever?"

"It seems worth getting right."

"Is it?" Witch-Hazel asked archly. "Do you even know if the unicorn will let your hive live here? It's her grove. Have you asked?"

Zwi stopped hovering above the rose bush and landed on one of the shadowy blossoms, literally taken aback by Witch-Hazel's question. "I haven't asked. Do you think ... you think she wouldn't let us live here? There are no other bees ... surely, her grove would benefit from a honeybee hive!"

Witch-Hazel wondered idly what it meant that there were no other bees in this vision the unicorn had glamoured for them. Were they too hard for her to fake, because Zwi would be more closely attuned to any mistakes they made? Or maybe, Zwi didn't actually like being around other bees, so Gloaming hadn't created any.

Maybe that was part of why Zwi and Witch-Hazel got along so well. Neither of them felt like they belonged with their own kind.

Witch-Hazel hated what she was about to suggest, because she didn't want to draw attention to herself and Mercy trying to sneak out of the grove. But she couldn't leave her friend here without trying to free her, and she couldn't think of any other way to convince her to let go of the tantalizing promise implied by these trees. "It can't hurt to ask, right?" She said the words softly, wishing she wasn't saying them at all. "Ask Gloaming if your hive can join you here, maybe to help you choose between the trees—"

"Oh, my hive can't come until I've picked one! A lowly worker scout such as myself could never ask the Queen's Highness to travel across the countryside—"

"To a grove filled with suitable trees? Really? You can't ask your queen to do that? Would it really be an imposition, or do you just want to keep the fun and glory of picking the tree for yourself?"

"Well … maybe …" Zwi admitted. She pawed at the petals of the rose she was perched on with her six talons. Except, they weren't ruby red rose petals; they were just plain drab green leaves, a little brown around the edges, wearing the shadow of a rose.

"Ask Gloaming," Witch-Hazel insisted. "And ... if anything goes wrong ... Mercy and I will be climbing the beanstalk. You can always join us. Always."

Witch-Hazel imagined a future where Zwi's hive settled in a new tree, and she built herself a nest in a neighboring tree. She could stay friends with Zwi, and become friends with her sister bees. But not here. Not in the unicorn's enchanted grove of lies.

12

Zwi wished Witch-Hazel and Mercy goodbye, telling them to stop by the grove and see her hive on their way back down the beanstalk. Surely, she'd have chosen a tree, and the new hive would be all settled by then.

Witch-Hazel agreed, half-heartedly. She hoped to never return to this land of shadows. And she doubted Zwi would ever rejoin her hive. The bee hadn't even been willing to promise to ask Gloaming about her hive joining her here.

Witch-Hazel feared that as soon as she was out of sight, the shadows would engulf Zwi, and she'd dance with imaginary ant drones for the rest of her life.

But Witch-Hazel couldn't save everyone. She'd be lucky to save herself. She could already feel the pull of the unicorn's shadows calling to her, growing brighter and more vivid in her vision. She had to focus very hard on her memories of Fish-Breath to stave them away, and even so, she found herself stumbling through mazes of brilliantly colored rose bushes—non-existent yet dazzling—as she worked her way toward the beanstalk in the middle of the grove.

The closer she got to the beanstalk, the more insistent the visions became. Brighter, more colorful roses. Butterflies and ladybugs singing and dancing together. Carnelian carrying a picnic basket in her mouth, overflowing with delicious delectables.

A handsome river otter, wearing a perfectly tailored suit—dripping as if he'd just finished splashing in a lake—held out his arm, as if asking Witch-Hazel to take it …

She almost tripped over her own feet at the sight of him. He looked like Fish-Breath. Exactly like Fish-Breath. She didn't think that was a mistake. But this time, she didn't think it was a vision Fish-Breath had sent to her, guiding her to find him; she knew it was yet another distraction, trying to stop her.

When Witch-Hazel managed to stumble her way past the shadow of an otter, suddenly all the shadows dropped away. The grove became a simple grove of fruit and nut trees. No illusions. And the beanstalk, thicker around than the biggest redwood tree, was almost within reach.

But suddenly, Witch-Hazel was so overcome with sadness and futility, her feet couldn't hold her up. She fell to the ground and lay on the soft grass like a squirrel who'd been shot with an arrow straight through the heart.

She ached. Not a real, physical ache. But one that pervaded her mind, making her body feel heavy.

She would never find Fish-Breath.

She couldn't free Zwi.

She'd raised a butterfly … but why? No one wanted the strange were-moth sitting on her shoulder, disguised as a swallowtail.

Even if Witch-Hazel did make it to the beanstalk, climb into the sky, and find Fish-Breath … would he be happy to see her? Perhaps she had imagined their connection. Perhaps he'd never felt as deeply for her, as she did for him.

Or worse, maybe she didn't have feelings for him. Maybe she was only imagining them in retrospect, giving herself an excuse for the same depression and unhappiness she'd struggled with her whole life.

She'd never been good at being a squirrel, so she'd imagined that she'd fallen in love with an otter. But when she came face to face with him, what if he didn't make her happy? What if his usually joyous face with his big, funny, oval nose and sparkly eyes simply creased with displeasure at the sight of her? And her own heart shriveled, realizing she'd wasted so much time on a wild goose chase.

Better to lie here forever, on the soft grass in a unicorn's grove, only inches away from a technicolor world of dreams, simply waiting to make her happy.

Witch-Hazel's world shrunk down to an awareness of her own breathing and a numb attempt to ignore the voices in her brain, screaming horrible things at her.

Then a bright, shining, slice of mother-of-pearl cut across her sideways view of grass and trees. Witch-Hazel glanced up without moving and saw Gloaming standing above her, head low, and spiraling horn pointing at the yellow butterfly still perched on the sad, sad squirrel's shoulder.

"Your ward has emerged from her chrysalis," Gloaming said.

"Cocoon," Witch-Hazel corrected. There was no point in hiding the truth. There was no point in anything. "Are you doing this to me? Making me feel this way? Is it a punishment for rejecting your glamours?"

"I could stab my horn through your heart if I wanted to punish you," Gloaming observed.

The unicorn looked just as beautiful, glowing, and ethereal as ever. Peaceful and serene.

Danger doesn't always look like sharp teeth, glinting in the dark of night.

"Or trample you with my hooves. You're very small." The unicorn's hooves were cloven and shined like crescent moons, and her legs stretched up like four saplings. A whole miniature grove of stompy unicorn feet.

The yellow butterfly on Witch-Hazel's shoulder took flight, as lightly as a bubble rising. Mercy floated to the tip of Gloaming's horn, where Zwi had been perched when Witch-Hazel first saw her.

Mercy landed on the horn, and Gloaming lifted her head, raising the perfect yellow butterfly into the sky. Her swallowtail wings looked like pieces of sunlight, cut into fancy shapes, and laid across the dappled blue peeking out between the ceiling of branches.

"You brought danger to my grove." Gloaming's voice wavered, sounding uncertain for the first time. "And I didn't see it." She raised her front right hoof, looking unsteady, ready to break and run, as if a fire were chasing her. "I'm too late."

"Too late?" Witch-Hazel asked, pressing a paw into the grass, pivoting herself, and lifting herself up. She shook out her tail, feeling twitchy and quivery all over.

Suddenly, Witch-Hazel didn't know why she'd been lying there on the ground; why all those feelings had felt so certain and pressing. She would find out her feelings for Fish-Breath and discover whether he returned feelings for her when she found him. The uncertainty didn't matter. He was her friend, and it was right to look for him.

Witch-Hazel put a paw to her head, feeling dizzy from the way her entire perspective had shifted in a moment. "You've released me from your enchantment …"

"It stopped working," Gloaming corrected. She scratched at the ground with a cloven hoof, tearing at the grass. "A magic more powerful than mine is in play."

"What do you mean?"

The unicorn shook her head, causing her mane to sway. The downy white tresses looked like cirrus clouds stretched out across a summer sky. Soft as fresh cotton blowing in the wind.

"You don't know?"

Could it be the All-Being? Witch-Hazel wondered. Fish-Breath had sent a vision of himself to guide her to the air lilies she would need … Could he have interceded on her behalf here somehow?

"I had hoped you would stay for longer," Gloaming said. "It gets lonely guarding the only path to the All-Being's castle. No one comes anymore."

"You kept us here because you're lonely?" After an initial burst of outrage, it occurred to Witch-Hazel that she might have misjudged the unicorn: maybe Gloaming would let Zwi bring her hive here. A whole hives of bees would be a lot more company.

"You're wondering whether I've been leading your friend the honeybee on a merry chase, a hollow pursuit, letting her spend weeks choosing between trees that I'd never let her hive settle in."

"Well, have you?"

The unicorn had the decency to look ashamed. But even shame looked beautiful on her. "Yes. My magic is strong enough to keep a few visitors here safely … but I couldn't control an entire hive of honeybees living here, scouting daily, flying miles to fetch pollen for their honey."

"So what? Why must you *control* them?"

"Coming and going? Leading other creatures here? No, no, they'd fray the fabric of the protection spell I've woven. The beanstalk would wither and fall. I wouldn't be able to protect it against that kind of … decay."

A coldness grabbed Witch-Hazel's heart. Decay. That's what it had looked like in the amber vision when all those highways between the earth and sky fell—the world was decaying. This beanstalk had only been protected from the decay plaguing the earth because of a lonely, selfish unicorn's magic. But was it selfish for her to want company? She was keeping vigil, and no one should be alone forever, surrounded by only their dreams for company.

Witch-Hazel almost felt guilty for pressuring Zwi to see through the unicorn's lies. The bee had been happy, flitting from tree to tree, imagining futures that would never come to pass. But … it wasn't Zwi's fault the unicorn was lonely. This wasn't Zwi's vigil. And her hive was counting on her to find a tree and return.

At least … Zwi believed they were. Witch-Hazel wondered. Zwi had been gone for so long, and beehives have many workers and scouts. What if her hive had already found a new tree and moved on without her? Or what if they'd dwindled and died with their dying tree?

What if when Zwi finally found a tree, and returned home with her joyous news, she found nothing but an

Mary E. Lowd

empty, abandoned, derelict hive waiting for her? A memorial to her sisters, but none of the sisters themselves.

These were sad thoughts, and Witch-Hazel didn't like them. All she knew for sure was that Zwi was her friend, and they still had quests to finish together. "Where is Zwi?" she asked.

The unicorn trotted away, fetched a sprig of leaves from a nearby shrub, and after biting the sprig off, carried it back to Witch-Hazel. She lowered her head, offering the cluster of emerald, spade-shaped leaves to the squirrel.

Witch-Hazel took them. Zwi clung to the stem of the mid-most leaf, sound asleep, and snoring with a soft buzz. Most likely dreaming of a beautiful future for her hive.

"I cast a sleeping spell on her," Gloaming said.

"She'll be furious when she wakes up." Witch-Hazel wasn't sure if it was better to wake Zwi now, or wait until she'd climbed high enough in the beanstalk to get fully away from the pull of the unicorn's magic.

"Not my problem now." The unicorn turned tail and trotted away. Just because a mythical creature is beautiful and magical, it doesn't mean they have to be gracious or forgiving.

Witch-Hazel still felt hurt. She had been friends with Carnelian, and that fox had been a representation of Gloaming's magic—in some small way, a piece or reflection of Gloaming.

She shouldn't feel guilty for leaving a creature who had tricked and fooled her ... but she did. Regret and confusion clung to Witch-Hazel's heart as she slipped the cluster of emerald leaves into her backpack on top of the bed of air lilies, returned the pack to her shoulders, and—after calling to Mercy to follow her—scurried fast as she could to the base of the beanstalk.

At the last moment, Witch-Hazel slowed down and placed her claws on the beanstalk reverentially. The emerald flesh didn't give under her claws the way she expected. It was unyielding and tough like the bark of a tree, even though it looked soft and smooth like the flesh of a young plant.

But of course, the beanstalk was old. Older than Witch-Hazel's grandparents, and probably their grand-parents. It was ancient, and it was hard. But squirrel claws are sharp and designed for climbing. Even if the emerald flesh didn't yield pleasingly under them, Witch-Hazel's spiky claws clung tight, and she scrambled up the base of the beanstalk—a veritable wall of green. Broad, wide, tall ... it seemed to go on forever.

Forever and ever. Upward into the sky.

Witch-Hazel felt the exhaustion in her shoulders first. Then she noticed that her paws had started to feel numb. How long had she been climbing? Hours? Except, the morning sun was still low in the sky.

The fruit and nut trees of the unicorn's grove had fallen behind her, turning into a mere carpet of green in the distance, long ago. She had begun climbing on the sunward side of the stalk, but eventually she couldn't stand the heat of the sunlight burning against her back, making the backpack an uncomfortable heat trap over her fur. So, she scrambled sideways, traveling around the beanstalk in a spiral, until she came to its side—half light, half shadow. A much more comfortable mix.

But still, she would need more than the flat trunk of a beanstalk eventually. She couldn't climb a flat surface forever, clinging tightly with her claws. She'd grow exhausted, and she feared she'd already traveled too far to make it back down before exhaustion took over and she fell.

Falling from such a height would be instant death. Even for squirrels, who are so good at jumping they can almost fly.

And yet the cloud with the All-Being's castle remained so far above Witch-Hazel that no matter how she craned her neck and squinted her eyes and clung to hope ... she couldn't believe that the trip upward would be shorter than several days of climbing. How had Fish-Breath meant for her to reach him? Not like this ... She hadn't even reached the height where she would need the air lilies yet.

She couldn't climb for days without stopping. She wouldn't last. She needed a place to rest, or a way back down that wouldn't kill her.

Once again, Witch-Hazel had rushed headlong into a situation that should have required careful consideration. And this time, she feared it might be her end.

13

WITCH-HAZEL STOPPED CLIMBING. She had run out of hope. And if she'd been alone, she might have clung there—bewildered by the audacity that had brought her there and trapped by her own uncertainty about going forward—until exhaustion wiped her consciousness away, replacing intolerable awareness of her untenable position with the blessed release of sleep. And her body would have fallen, a mere scrap of gray, a used up rag of squirrel, falling, falling, falling …

Could Gloaming revive the dead? The snake had been able to … But zombies seemed less like a unicorn's style.

Perhaps roused by the sudden cessation in movement, Zwi climbed out of the backpack, out from under the flap covering its top, and perched on Witch-Hazel's shoulder, sleepiness still making her antennae waggle groggily.

"Good morning," Mercy sang with a fluting voice from Witch-Hazel's other shoulder.

The squirrel was so surprised to hear her butterfly ward speak that she almost lost her grip on the beanstalk. Mercy had been floating and fluttering alongside her, occasionally stopping to perch on her shoulder, all morning long, and had shown no signs of wanting to speak—or even knowing how to—before.

Zwi sounded surprised too as she buzzed, "Good morning," back to the butterfly.

A long moment passed in silence while Witch-Hazel avoided blurting out something stupid like, "You speak!" or "Is it normal for caterpillars to not talk?" She didn't want to make it weird for Mercy now that she finally was speaking; she wouldn't want the butterfly to feel embarrassed and stop. And besides, how could Mercy know what was normal for other caterpillars? She'd never met one. As far as Witch-Hazel knew, none of the three of them had.

Fortunately, Zwi saved Witch-Hazel from her fatigued, tongue-tied stupidity by saying, "We're far above the grove."

"Yes," Witch-Hazel agreed. Her claws ached. She shouldn't be able to feel her claws, but still, they ached.

"I fell asleep …" Zwi sounded like she was still lost in the unicorn's illusions.

"Gloaming cast a sleeping spell on you."

"She wouldn't answer my question … the one you insisted I ask."

"It was all fake," Witch-Hazel said bitterly.

"Not all of it," Mercy chimed in. "You were real."

Once again, the butterfly's voice stopped both of her caretakers cold. They'd grown so used to her silence, they didn't know how to respond to her words.

"Why did you stop climbing?" Mercy asked, all child-like innocence. She was truly a butterfly freshly emerged from her chrysalis—born into adulthood that very day. "Fish-Breath is waiting for you."

"What?" Witch-Hazel exclaimed, surprised that Mercy knew about Fish-Breath. But then she remembered all the late nights in the weeping willow when she would ramble about her hopes and dreams to a quietly leaf-munching caterpillar in her backpack. Mercy had shown no sign she'd been listening. Apparently, she had been.

Zwi chuckled, a staccato buzz. But then she added, "Yes, it's a good question. Why have you stopped? There's a long way to go."

Frustrated, exhausted, and angry, Witch-Hazel shouted, "I'm tired! Okay? I've been climbing for hours, with no one to talk to, just my own fears yelling at me, and my shoulders ache; my paws ache; even my *claws* ache, and if I don't find a place to rest soon …" Her voice got very small before finishing the sentence. "… I'm going to fall."

"Why don't you rest on one of the leaves?" Mercy asked.

Witch-Hazel blinked.

Zwi's antennae rotated in little circles, showing she was just as boggled by the question. And then they both blurted: "What leaves?"

Witch-Hazel was deeply relieved somehow that Zwi didn't know what Mercy was talking about either. For a moment, she'd felt like she was losing her mind. But then, at the suggestion that there were leaves around her, she started to see them. Translucent, ethereal, daydream leaves as big as dinnerplates and thicker than mushroom caps.

Maybe she really was losing her mind.

"Gloaming enchanted them," Zwi buzzed. "So we couldn't see them, didn't she?"

Witch-Hazel sputtered inarticulately. She could have been stopping to rest all along! But that dratted unicorn had lied to her one more time, trying to convince her to turn back.

The joke was on the unicorn. Witch-Hazel had wanted so badly to escape the grove's illusions and make it to the All-Being's castle that she'd climbed too high to turn back, before even realizing the imaginary danger Gloaming had tried to threaten her with.

With shaky paws, Witch-Hazel climbed onto the flat, friendly surface of the nearest leaf—there were so many of them! She must have been climbing around them for hours, instinctively avoiding them as obstacles, without realizing what she was doing. Such a sneaky, deceptive spell. If Witch-Hazel had any doubts about the unicorn's duplicity—any secret sympathy for her—before, then this final barb of illusions washed them away.

Gloaming deserved to be alone in her grove.

Blessed rest!

Witch-Hazel had only been awake since before dawn, but she'd had a good night's sleep before that. So, she wasn't sleepy. Just physically tired. And now that she knew she could stop to rest when she needed to, she didn't feel as dangerously exhausted. After a few minutes of rest—maybe a quarter of an hour—she found herself itching to climb again.

This time, as Witch-Hazel climbed, Zwi buzzed along beside her, gently engaging Mercy in conversation, subtly pushing the butterfly into getting more comfortable talking. They talked about the grove and Gloaming's deceptions, which Zwi seemed more sympathetic to than Witch-Hazel felt after spending much of the morning fearing she'd fall to her death. They talked about the sisterhood of butterflies and moths who kept the fairy rings, at least, what little Zwi knew about them. And they talked about the All-Being's castle—why they were traveling there, what Zwi knew about it from legends passed down through song and dance among her people, and what the All-Being might be able to do for Mercy.

Zwi hoped the All-Being could stabilize Mercy's form—freezing her into being either a butterfly or moth, without switching between the two anymore. But Mercy wasn't sure she wanted that. She'd been a fluctuating creature her entire life, and she didn't see why she should change.

Witch-Hazel was inclined to agree with Mercy, but she spoke very little as they climbed.

Climbing with paws and claws clinging to the twisting flesh of a beanstalk seemed to require more energy than simply flying alongside it. Witch-Hazel began to suspect that some of her exhaustion from earlier had stemmed from intuitively avoiding leaves and navigating the uneven surface of the beanstalk without having a conscious awareness of what she'd been doing. For the beanstalk didn't have a simple, flat surface. Perhaps at the very base, down in the grove, it had been a singular trunk. But somewhere along the way, the stalk had split into a multitude of twisting vines, twining around each other.

Witch-Hazel had left Gloaming's grove too quickly to pack any food in her backpack, but fortunately, the beanstalk provided easy meals. Any time she felt hungry, it was simple work to find ripe beans. She could sit on a leaf, crack them open, eat the tender kernels inside, and then munch on the crunchy pod. She never knew what kind of beans she'd find inside a pod—red, yellow, green; wide and flat or round and dimpled. They tasted different too. Some were sweet, others meaty.

Zwi and Mercy were able to drink nectar from the tiny flowers—pink, red, and yellow; shaped like trumpets and clamshells—that grew in colorful sprays all over the vine.

Dusk lasted a long time as the distant sun sank beneath the horizon. When the final sliver of the sun's golden disk slipped out of sight, Mercy landed on Witch-Hazel's shoulder, shaking and quaking, and her body transformed. Her slender, tiger-striped thorax and abdomen thickened, paled, and grew shaggy with white fur. Her long black legs turned pink, and her antennae feathered. Her wings lost their stripes, and gained dreamy false eyes. Bright yellow and black changed to dusky green.

"Does it hurt?" Witch-Hazel asked. "When you change form?"

Mercy was silent for a long time before answering, and Witch-Hazel feared her question had been out of place. But then the Luna moth on her shoulder said, "I hadn't thought about whether it hurt. It just happens. Every day, it happens. It's what existing feels like. But … yes. I guess it is painful."

Witch-Hazel shivered, and she wasn't sure whether it was from the haunting tone of Mercy's voice or the chill in the air now that the sun was down.

The stars looked brighter now that they were so high in the sky, and Witch-Hazel kept climbing late into the night. As a squirrel, she was used to sleeping in trees, high above the ground. But not this high. And somehow, losing consciousness when the ground was so far away that it felt like part of an entirely different world felt ... unsafe. Unanchored. Yet the anchor she was traveling toward was closer to the stars in the sky than the earth of the ground below.

When Witch-Hazel finally did sleep, closer to dawn than dusk, she dreamed of Fish-Breath. In her sleep, she and Fish-Breath had rejoined paths long ago, and he was already showing her around the city of Riverton. He made dinner for her, and in the way of dreams, she knew it was delicious without quite knowing what it was or actually having to eat it. Then the two of them met with Twiggy, the beaver who'd been traveling with him when they all met. The clever beaver showed off the crazy inventions she tinkered with inside the cozy home inside her dam. Strange devices built from sticks and stones.

Witch-Hazel awoke feeling even more determined to climb quickly and steadily up the beanstalk than when she'd fallen asleep. The part of her dream that haunted her didn't have to do with Fish-Breath—they had parted on good terms. She had sacrificed her own goals and treasures to save his life. But Twiggy ...

After Fish-Breath had ascended with wings given to him by the All-Being, Witch-Hazel had tried to reach out to Twiggy—to offer comfort and take some in return. But Twiggy had blamed her for their shared loss, and the beaver had struck out on her own, refusing to continue traveling together.

Witch-Hazel hadn't realized how badly she craved Twiggy's forgiveness. But the dream had lifted the recriminations and hurt between them, allowing Witch-Hazel to feel the lightness of being friends again. Even if only briefly. She liked that feeling.

She climbed onward.

14

Halfway through the second day of climbing, Witch-Hazel began to pass abandoned bird nests, nestled in the crannies between the beanstalk vines, and she heard chittering, chattering, and squawks above, breaking the eerie white noise of the wind sighing past.

She also noticed a colorful speck in the distance. At first, she thought her eyes were playing tricks on her, but the bright speck kept growing from a mere imperfection in the rich blue of the sky to a small coin of color. It looked like a rainbow had curled up into a little ball and was floating aimlessly through the sky like a soap bubble.

Witch-Hazel liked sneaking glances over her shoulder at the colorful spot as she climbed. She was afraid to mention it to Zwi or Mercy, because it seemed too strange to be real. She'd already been having visions of Fish-Breath and her mind had played tricks on her for a month in the unicorn's garden. She no longer trusted her senses. And the colorful spot seemed less likely to be real than to be another trick. But she liked looking at it. She liked how it gave a focus to the amorphous, ever-changing landscape of tousled silver clouds in the blue around her. It felt like an anchor. And she didn't want it to disappear when she mentioned it, the way the illusion hiding the beanstalk's leaves had.

Around noon, Mercy took a break from flying. She perched on the flap over the top of Witch-Hazel's backpack and let the squirrel carry her upward. Witch-Hazel didn't mind. Mercy was as light as a flower, and she already had a backpack stuffed full of those.

Zwi flew on ahead. She was a scout, used to scouting, and the idea of checking the path ahead before Witch-Hazel got there seemed to make her happy. Witch-Hazel wasn't sure what Zwi could possibly learn that would be worth reporting back—the beanstalk made for a very simple, straightforward path—but it also couldn't hurt.

Witch-Hazel sang a song from her childhood to pass the time and entertain Mercy:

> "Tree to tree,
> Branch to branch,
> The weight of the world,
> Can't hold us down,
>
> "Leap and jump,
> Climb and fly,
> The trees are alive,
> When squirrels are around,

"Chase and flee,
Follow and run,
You can't catch me,
But I'll catch you,
Before we're done!"

Witch-Hazel meant to keep singing for Mercy, but the song had taken her back so far into her childhood that she hardly noticed when she was done singing. She was too busy remembering games of tag that ranged all through the oak copse. She'd never been good at catching her littermates, but she had been good at running from them. She'd been fast, but easily tricked by her siblings feinting and dodging.

"Do squirrels dance?" Mercy asked in her piping voice.

"Sure," Witch-Hazel said. "Sometimes."

"What are your dances about?"

Witch-Hazel's ears pricked up in surprise at the question. "About? Oh, you mean, like Zwi's dances. Squirrels don't dance like that. We just … dance. Shaking our tails, shuffling our feet, moving for fun. It doesn't mean anything. Except maybe that we're happy. Not like when bees dance."

Witch-Hazel wished she could see Mercy's face, because the butterfly got very quiet in response to her answer. Of course, she supposed she might not be able to glean much meaning from the curl of Mercy's proboscis or the tilt of her antennae. Mercy had only had a proboscis and antennae for a day now, and that wasn't much time for Witch-Hazel to learn how to read emotion and expression in them. She'd learned some rudimentary understanding of Mercy's caterpillar features—the way her mouth parts clenched up or wiggled; the way her green skin had wrinkled or smoothed. She'd be able to see meaning there.

But Mercy's butterfly face was still inscrutable. Yet she wanted to see it, because she wanted to learn. She wanted to connect with this young creature she'd been caring for all these weeks. Because even in Gloaming's world of illusions, Mercy had been real. And it troubled Witch-Hazel that Mercy's metamorphosis felt like it had wiped away the connection between them.

Rationally, Witch-Hazel knew that the tiger swallowtail on her back was the same person as the chubby green caterpillar. But in her heart … it felt like the caterpillar was gone, and the butterfly was an interloper who'd only arrived in her life yesterday.

Zwi returned from scouting, literally buzzing with news. "The birds above! A colony of ravens! Chased me! Tried to eat me! But then they gave me a warning … and a challenge …"

Zwi was whipping around Witch-Hazel so erratically, so quickly that the squirrel kept turning her head to keep the flying honeybee in sight, but she couldn't keep up.

"Slow down," she said. "Land on a leaf maybe? I'm going to fall down the beanstalk trying to keep track of you like this."

"But … her dancing," Mercy said.

"Dancing?" Witch-Hazel asked. All she had seen was fitful, volatile flying that seemed to express restlessness and urgency. Nothing more.

Had Zwi been speaking dance just then? And could Mercy understand the dancing language of bees? Witch-Hazel supposed that Mercy had spent her caterpillar phase watching Zwi dance just as much as listening to the two of them speak. Somehow, it hadn't occurred to her though that the caterpillar had been learning two languages.

Zwi landed on the edge of a broad leaf, just as Witch-Hazel had requested, bringing whatever dance she'd been doing to a halt.

"She was telling you all about the warning!" Mercy said. "Didn't you want to know more?"

"I do …" Witch-Hazel said, cautiously. "But I can't understand Zwi's dances. They're pretty, but … I don't know that language."

Mercy lifted off from where she'd perched on Witch-Hazel's back and fluttered around to land on the broad leaf beside Zwi. She stared at Witch-Hazel with her inscrutable face—proboscis curled tightly and antennae tilted at a low angle. Witch-Hazel didn't know for sure, but the expression seemed to be disapproving, as if Mercy were questioning how foolish she could be for not under-standing a language that a caterpillar had learned in a few weeks.

But surely, a baby caterpillar's brain is more elastic, more suited to learning new languages, than an adult squirrel's …

And yet, Witch-Hazel did feel foolish. If she were cleverer, she'd have been paying closer attention during the many months she'd traveled with Zwi. Maybe she could have picked up something from Zwi's dances, a rudimentary understanding. Instead, she'd simply assumed it was a language that was forever out of reach to her, because she didn't have the wings and extra legs to speak with it. But she could have listened.

Witch-Hazel climbed from the vines she'd been cling-ing to onto another broad leaf, just slightly below the one where the two insects were perched. She settled down, curling her tail around her like a shawl. It was getting colder as they got higher in the sky. Then she said, "I'm sorry for interrupting your dance, Zwi. Will you tell me about the warning?"

Zwi stayed perched on the leaf, not returning to her dance. And Witch-Hazel felt guilty for that. She had interrupted something meaningful, even if she hadn't understood the meaning, and now it was over. Zwi spoke only in words. She said, "They asked me if I would hazard the maze of twigs, buying passage through the ravens' colony with promises, and then seek the treasure they'd lost, risking the deathly talons above."

"Cryptic," Witch-Hazel observed wryly. She'd only interacted closely with a raven once before, and that raven had been a mad creature, living in an underground library, guarding the books with her life and issuing all kinds of weird threats and warnings.

Witch-Hazel was not fond of ravens.

"What did you answer them?" Mercy asked.

"I told them yes," Zwi said. "When a bird gives you a choice between being eaten or promising them … anything. You make the promise and worry about the repercussions later." Her antennae dipped down as she looked up at Witch-Hazel. "I told them I'd need your help, and we'd return together to complete their quest."

"More quests," Witch-Hazel said. "Quests upon quests. Side quests and main quests. Upward quests and downward quests. Some day, it would be nice to do something other than go on quests."

But today was not that day, and so Witch-Hazel kept climbing. Glancing up and down the beanstalk, she judged that she'd made it halfway to where the green highway of vines disappeared into the clouds above. She could see nothing of the castle from her vision in the amber. Just puffy, crenulated white.

Another day and half, maybe two days of climbing. Or longer if the ravens caused too much trouble. Then she could disappear into the clouds, enter the castle, and be rejoined with Fish-Breath.

So she kept climbing. The chattering of the ravens grew louder, and decorations appeared, twined into the vines, or hanging from the leaves. Bits of metal and glass. Shiny things. Rusty bent forks, broken bottles as green as emeralds, and colorful bits of flaccid plastic hanging from ribbons from long-since popped balloons.

Witch-Hazel didn't know if all ravens were collectors, but the librarian under the earth had been deeply possessive of her books and the colony of ravens in the beanstalk had a very clear interest in shiny, colorful objects.

When Witch-Hazel made it to the first actual nest, she saw a raven settled inside the artfully arranged cluster of twigs, watching her with sparkling black eyes. The raven was larger than her—larger than the largest of squirrels— but not by much.

Witch-Hazel relaxed at the sight of the bird, realizing that she'd let Zwi's fear of the ravens get to her. But of course, the ravens were far more of a threat to a tiny bee who could be snapped up by a sharp obsidian beak in one bite than to a squirrel nearly their size.

Sure, in a fight, Witch-Hazel would be at a disadvantage without wings, especially this high from the ground. But she'd hold her own. Besides, she was a battle-hardened traveler at this point, and for all of Zwi's fear, the bee was small and fast. She could elude the ravens' sight and speed past them.

The two of them had fought their way through an army of zombies. A few ravens collecting lost scraps of metal and bits of ribbon? Not a real threat.

But then Mercy landed lightly on Witch-Hazel's shoulder, and she remembered that she had more to worry about than herself and Zwi—they had a ward to protect. And right now, during daylight, that ward was a dazzling array of yellow and black stripes with gemlike bits of red and blue. A shiny prize to be sure. And her wings were far too delicate for her to hide inside the confines of the backpack anymore … Unlike Zwi, who crawled under the backpack's top flap to hide from the piercing gaze of the raven. Witch-Hazel sighed deeply. Then she introduced herself to the raven who'd been watching them curiously.

"My name is Witch-Hazel," she said, "and my companion, Zwi the bee, has already negotiated safe passage through your colony for our crew, which includes the butterfly on my shoulder. Her name is Mercy."

Mercy flapped her wings, slowly and silently. She said nothing.

The raven tilted her head, eying the silent butterfly. She clacked her beak in a way that seemed … hungry but restrained. "Very well, champion," she said. "See that you return our book to us unharmed. Don't go pulling any pages out for yourself."

"Of course," Witch-Hazel agreed amiably. She began climbing again before the conversation could become any more awkward. Though, she had a lot of questions. For better and worse, she passed many more ravens along the way. Each of them eyed Mercy in a way that made Witch-Hazel deeply uncomfortable, and one by one, they revealed snippets of information about her new quest, without the squirrel even having to ask.

Apparently, an eagle with a massive nest above the raven colony had stolen their sacred book, *The Crownomicon*. The ravens wanted it back. That was all. A nice, simple, straightforward quest. Steal back a book from a gigantic bird with a hooked beak, massive talons, and a short temper that had the entire colony of ravens all fluttery and uncertain.

For a brief while, Witch-Hazel toyed with the idea of ignoring Zwi's promise to the ravens. Once she'd made it past the eagle's nest, what would stop her from simply continuing onward? Never returning with the book? There must be another way down from the All-Being's castle … and if not, well, that was a problem for later. After she had Fish-Breath by her side once again.

But as she passed ravens—in their nests; twining colorful ribbon through the beanstalk vines; hopping from leaf to leaf; and flapping distractingly in the air beside her—each with a clever quip or cryptic comment, it became abundantly clear that a group of them planned to meet her above the eagle's nest and extract either a sacred book from her paws … or blood from her body.

What was it about ravens and books?

This book, apparently, was a powerful spell book, and the more Witch-Hazel learned about the spells that the ravens had been using from it—fire spells to cast beautiful but noisy firework shows for themselves; water spells to make it suddenly begin raining over the eagle's nest; and wind spells to let themselves coast through the air, riding the gusts like a rollercoaster and perhaps also knocking chunks of twigs out of the eagle's nest—the more sympathy Witch-Hazel felt for the eagle. Nonetheless, she didn't think her sympathy would be returned by the eagle if she tried to steal the spell book back from its nest.

She would soon face either an angry eagle or a murder of angry crows. Well, ravens. Witch-Hazel wasn't entirely clear on the difference. She suspected that it had more to do with the mood of the bird talking to her than anything more fundamental—a big black bird was a raven when it wanted to be seen as mysterious or threatening to a squirrel, and a crow when it wanted be seen as jovial, jocular, and fun to be around.

Crows would hang out with a traveling squirrel, telling jokes and shooting the breeze. Maybe share a few toasted chestnuts. But somehow it was always ravens kicking her

out of underground libraries or sending her after mysterious spell books.

15

THERE WAS A PATCH of bare vine between the loosely grouped clusters of raven nests and the massive eagle nest above. No decorations. No colorful ribbons or bits of scrap metal glinting in the sun. A no one's land between the colony of jokesters and their stern, serious neighbor.

Witch-Hazel didn't miss avoiding the decorations as she climbed. To her, they'd seemed gaudy and overdone. But she did miss the sense that the eagle's nest was still far above her. With every leap upward, she came closer to the intimidating thicket of twigs and branches, clumped together into a giant lump that circled the entire beanstalk. It made her think of the one beaver dam she'd ever seen. Except, instead of blocking the course of a stream of water, this nest blocked the course of a stream of vine.

She would have to find a way through the clusters of twigs, or she'd have to climb outward, away from the beanstalk, around the bulbous curve of the nest. Witch-Hazel didn't like the idea of climbing into a giant predator's home … but she couldn't steal back *The Crownomicon* if she didn't. Besides, each glance over her shoulder, downward, told her that it wasn't safe to climb outward from the vine, trusting twigs to hold firmly together. She couldn't afford to fall from this height.

She'd been climbing for nearly two days. The world below looked like nothing she'd ever seen before—entire forests had become nothing more than stippled patches of dark green; fields and meadows were smoother patches of spring green and gold; and lakes were mere puddles. Rivers snaked through the different patterns of green like cracks in the world. The entire journey she and Zwi had undertaken so far—everywhere they'd been, all of the places they'd traveled through—could be seen at once. Her whole life and all of her adventures were small enough to fit inside this single, expansive view.

And the current moment, while Witch-Hazezl clung to the side of a beanstalk, deciding what to do, was twisted by the perspective to seem as large as the whole panorama. Her heartbeat echoing in her ears and her breathing, a ragged rhythm, were as large to her up here as windstorms and the drumming of thunder would be below.

This was what birds saw every day when they flew. No wonder they could be so arrogant. To themselves, they seemed as large as the whole world, because they could remove themselves from it.

If she fell, Witch-Hazel wondered, how long would she fall for? Would her fluffy tail act like a parachute, slowing her descent? Could she spread her arms and glide like a flying squirrel or sugar glider? She didn't have webbing like them.

No, it wasn't safe. She'd have to climb through, not around.

But Mercy didn't need to come with her. Mercy could float past the dangerous eagle's nest without risking her delicate wings inside of it. Fortunately, twilight was falling, and better yet, a cloud had blown in on the wind, shrouding everything in a chilly, foggy mist that clung damply to Witch-Hazel's fur. She didn't like how the cloud made her shiver, or obscured her view of the inexplicable ball of rainbow floating in the distance. The rainbow ball had grown nearly as large as a full moon before the cloud blocked it from sight. Whatever it was—imaginary or real—it was getting closer.

But the cold fog of the cloud did mean that only a few feet away from the beanstalk, Mercy's bright tiger-striped wings—which would soon turn back to pale, lime green— would be obscured from view by layers and veils of silky white mist.

When Witch-Hazel reached the bottom of the eagle's nest, twigs making a gnarled ceiling above her pointed ears, she stopped and explained her plan: "Zwi, you're small and fast enough that I'd appreciate your help in scouting out the nest ahead of me as I climb through. But Mercy, you don't need to come with us. You should fly past the nest—fly away from the beanstalk first, far enough away that the eagle won't see you—and then find somewhere to perch and wait for us above."

Mercy had been floating alongside Witch-Hazel, but during the squirrel's speech, she stopped, landed on her shoulder, and perched there silently.

Zwi landed on the tip of one of the twigs hanging down from the eagle's nest.

Finally, with a gentle flap of her swallowtail wings, Mercy said, "I want to come with you."

"You'll be safer this way," Witch-Hazel urged.

"I've never been away from you."

Witch-Hazel didn't know what to say to that. She'd never really meant to become a mother on this journey, even a surrogate one.

"I wish I could hide in your backpack again."

The child-like wish to return to a place where one had once felt safe when younger was so simple and pure that it made Witch-Hazel's heart ache. The ache in her heart twisted up even further over the fact that the safe home this beautiful were-moth missed was nothing more than a beaten up old knapsack she'd been carrying on her back for months.

Mercy might have a mature butterfly's body, but she'd only emerged from her chrysalis two days ago. Compared to a battle-hardened squirrel and worker bee on their second big quest, she was still a child.

"Zwi, why don't you go with Mercy?" Witch-Hazel said. "I'll be fine on my own. In fact, I think it'll be simpler. Faster even, this way."

Zwi ran a talon along the length of her right antenna, while continuing to cling to the tip of the twig with her other five limbs. "I could scout first … while you two wait here."

Witch-Hazel shook her head. She didn't like the idea of Zwi going into the eagle's nest alone. The bee was smaller than bite-sized to a raven, let alone an eagle. "No, I don't think that's necessary. How hard can it be for me to find a book in a pile of twigs? I don't even know why I thought you should scout in the first place. Go on above, and I'll meet you both on the other side."

Zwi looked like she wanted to press Witch-Hazel further on the matter. The tilt of her antennae, sharply toward each other and down, suggested she was displeased. She would prefer scouting dangerous territory and seeking out treasures to babysitting a fearful butterfly. But she'd spent the last month growing attached to Mercy too, and if she pressed Witch-Hazel further, it would just make the young butterfly feel guilty for causing their disagreement.

Zwi bowed her head. "As you say. Come with me, Mercy. Let's find some flowers to feast on while Witch-Hazel finds the book."

The two yellow-and-black insects floated away into the darkening mist, bright points of contrast and color in an otherwise monochromatic sky turning darker and darker shades of gray. They danced with each other as they flew, Zwi leading Mercy, both of them speaking in a language Witch-Hazel still didn't understand.

And suddenly, Witch-Hazel found herself alone, facing a deadly challenge that stood between her and the end of her quest, which otherwise felt so very near.

"I wish Fish-Breath were here," she said, speaking to the mist or herself. She wasn't sure. Then she took the plunge and reached up into the cluster of twigs above her. She pulled at the twigs with her paws, yanking some out and dropping them in fistfuls down the beanstalk, and others she shoved aside, until she'd opened up a gap in the bottom of the nest, wide enough for a small squirrel to wiggle through.

As soon as Witch-Hazel pushed her head into the gap, she was overpowered by the smell: an acrid, sour scent of feathers and death. Witch-Hazel suddenly had a lot more sympathy for the trickster ravens and their annoying spells as she realized they must provide the main source of food for an eagle living so high up here.

A squirrel would look like food to the eagle as well. If she was lucky, the eagle was out flying, maybe hunting, right now. Second best, maybe the eagle was asleep. She'd have to be very quiet.

Perhaps ... she could wait until she'd seen the eagle leave?

But night had nearly fallen, and Witch-Hazel didn't think she could sleep so close to an eagle's nest. Too dangerous. She could feel the fear crawling under her skin, making her fur prickle. Surely that fear would keep her awake, and she couldn't afford to face this challenge even more worn out from a sleepless night. Better to hope the eagle was sleeping and proceed with utmost caution.

She continued climbing into the nest.

Witch-Hazel relied on her nose to lead the way, as she scrambled through the tightly packed twigs and clumps of moss that seemed to form the curving walls between entire, enclosed rooms inside the nest. The gaps between clusters of twigs felt like they formed a maze of their own, hidden in the nest's walls, much tighter than the labyrinth she'd traveled through underground. As she squeezed through, the twigs scraped against her fur, catching in the straps of her backpack.

The scent she followed was dusty and almost sweet, reminding her of the smell of the walls of old books in the mad raven's underground library. But it was only the wispiest note of a scent, lost in the miasma of other smells. The scent she avoided was musty, rich, and feathered. Almost overpowering. The eagle itself. A third scent confused her—fresh, new, and clean. She didn't know what that smell could be, and so she didn't know whether to avoid it or crawl towards it.

Curiosity got the better of her, and Witch-Hazel let herself be drawn through the dark, clawing, thickets of broken and braided twigs toward the fresh, clean, new scent.

The fresh scent was easier to follow than the faint hints of dust and sweetness. It was brighter, clearer, stronger. Though, the faint hints of dust and sweetness seemed like they might be coming from the same direction. When she finally managed to press her nose through a gap between twigs and find the source above her, it was smooth and warm against her nose. An eggshell.

Oh, holy hell, she was inside a mama eagle's nest, messing with her unhatched eggs.

Witch-Hazel had made a lot of foolish decisions in her life and found herself backed into a lot of dangerous corners, but she wasn't sure she'd ever felt more foolish or more profoundly in danger than this.

Yet, with some delicate scrabbling, Witch-Hazel managed to push enough of the twigs and moss between two of the large eggs aside—they were larger and more oblong than apples, maybe even larger than grapefruit—and the scent of dust and sweetness rushed into her nostrils. In the faint light of the dying, foggy twilight that leaked in through the cracks between twigs, she made out the shape of a book, propped open behind the clutch of eggs at the far side of the nursery room, as if the eagle mama had been reading magic spells to her unhatched babies as bedtime stories.

What a strange choice for bedtime stories. Perhaps the baby eagles would hatch from their nests with spells already memorized, and they'd fight back against the ravens. A war between wizard birds, high up in a beanstalk.

Witch-Hazel needed to get that book and get out of here, before the eagle mama, wherever she was hiding in this gigantic labyrinthine nest, came back to settle on her clutch of eggs. Based on the size of the eggs—bigger than Witch-Hazel herself if she curled into a ball—the eagle must be huge.

Every nerve in Witch-Hazel's body screamed at her to hold still, to freeze, that it wasn't safe to move as much as a single muscle in this place. But she overcame the fear filling her body, forcing her limbs to obey the willpower of her mind, and not the fear of her senses. Step by excruciating step, she climbed over the warm, ecru eggs until she was able to reach out and grab both sides of *The Crownomicon* with a paw. She was about to close the book, making it easier to carry—it would be too large to slip in her backpack—when she noticed the name of the spell it was opened to:

Clear Eyes—A Dyspellment of Yllusions Great & Small

Witch-Hazel's eyes widened. It was hard to read in the dim light, but that sounded like a spell she needed to learn.

She never wanted to be bamboozled like she had been in the unicorn's garden again. She felt an ache when she thought about Carnelian and their friendship ... a friendship that had been entirely imaginary, because the gentle red fox who loved a big white bunny had been nothing more than a shadow Witch-Hazel wanted to see.

Clear eyes were exactly what Witch-Hazel needed.

But first, she needed to get out of the eagle's nest with the book. In order to avoid losing the page, Witch-Hazel lifted the book over her head, holding it open, and draped it over her back like an awkward, stiff shawl. She held it in place with her left paw while using her right to help her climb upward. She couldn't disappear into the walls of the nest with the book on her back, but the gaps between the twigs in the ceiling showed stars. There might be a lot of rooms inside this labyrinthine, gigantic bird nest, but the nursery room seemed to be near the top. All she had to do was get out and keep climbing.

She was so close.

And then a shriek pierced the muffled silence of the nest. A shriek from behind Witch-Hazel, inside the nest with her. The shriek was so loud, it echoed in her ears after it ended, replacing the muffled silence with a dull ringing. Her heart rate sped, as if her heart wanted to leap out of her chest and run away on its own, leaving her behind to face the danger she'd courted without anything so delicate inside her breast.

But it couldn't.

Her heart was trapped inside her, forced to break when Fish-Breath had nearly died and then flown into the sky, leaving her behind; forced to wallow in the illusions of the unicorn's garden and then grow numb when those pretty visions were washed away like sandcastles too close to the waves; and now forced to pound in terror as Witch-Hazel turned and saw a great golden figure hunching behind her.

The eagle barely fit inside the nursery; her wings scraped against the ceiling of twigs and moss, half out-stretched, held at a menacing angle. Her feathers looked as sharp and shiny as metal, as if they'd been cut from a sheet of copper and filed down until they had ragged edges, ready to slice the throat of an unwitting squirrel. But it was the beak, hooked and sharp as a thorn, and the talons, large enough to encircle a squirrel's ribcage with room to spare, that struck terror into Witch-Hazel's pounding heart.

"A squirrel?" the eagle shrieked, piercing the air with her voice again. "Mad raven! Why come to me in the shape of a squirrel? It will make no difference! Squirrels die as easily as ravens do!" She lunged forward, leading with her hooked beak.

Witch-Hazel panicked and, letting go of the book so it balanced precariously on her back, tore at the twig-and-moss wall behind her. Her heart screamed that there was no time to climb—only to burrow directly outward and get out of this eagle's lair as fast as possible, in the most direct route available. Straight out. Straight through. She threw fistfuls of twigs and moss over her shoulder at the eagle, until her paws broke through.

Twigs and moss tumbled downward into the night, leaving a gash, a wound in the protective walls around the eagle's nursery, looking out on the starry sky.

The fog was gone, cleared away.

Cold wind blew through the hole, stinging the bare skin of Witch-Hazel's nose and the insides of her ears.

Her ears flattened, and the sharpness of the night air brought Witch-Hazel back to her senses. She couldn't jump. She'd tumble down like the twigs and moss. She couldn't escape this way at all. And she had no weapons at hand. No sword. No dagger. Only the heavy book, still draped over her back, weighing her down like a cloak of lead.

But she also had nothing to lose.

Whereas the eagle was surrounded by treasures.

Witch-Hazel lifted the book above her head, as high as she could hold it, and shrieked with all the air in her lungs, in a voice much smaller than the eagle's but still piercing enough to rend the quiet night: "Stay back, or I'll smash the book down on your eggs!"

The eagle paused in her approach, blinked, and seemed uncertain of her next move. Witch-Hazel needed to use that moment, that bare flicker of uncertainty, to her advantage, but there was nothing for her to do. Nowhere to go. She looked out at the night again, sparkling with stars outside the stuffy confines of the nest, and she wondered if she could manage to climb around the outside of the nest—but that had seemed unsafe before she'd climbed through its walls, seeing first hand how easily the twigs and moss pulled out. She'd fall for certain. And her path up was blocked now by the eagle's spread wings.

Then she saw a shadow in the sky, blocking out the diamond-like stars. Could it be? The colors were dimmed by darkness, but in the moon's half light, it looked like the rainbow ball that had been drifting closer all day, following her like a friend. It was beneath her … and the distance of an oak tree's height away. But she could make that jump. She didn't know what she was jumping to, but it had to be better than this.

And she could make that jump.

16

WITCH-HAZEL LEAPT into the night, holding the book above her like the least effective parachute in existence. She didn't glide gracefully. No, she tumbled head over tail; tail over head; pages fluttering uselessly around her and the heavy book cover weighting her down. And then she bounced.

The surface she'd hit was made of coarse, taut fabric, and when she bounced off it again, she let go of the spell book with one paw, scrabbling frantically with the claws of all three free paws to snag the fabric and grab purchase as it slid past her. Instead, she kept sliding as the rotund surface squished under her weight, distending and disforming, giving her nothing solid to grab onto. She was about to give up on holding the book—if she let it fall, she'd have an extra paw to grab with—when a voice from below called, "Tally ho! Who's up there? What're you doing to my balloon?"

"Help!" Witch-Hazel cried, still fighting the balloon's fabric as if it were a bucking bronco, trying to rid itself of a useless human rider. The bronco was winning, having pushed Witch-Hazel all the way to the side. She was about to fall again, this time with nothing below her, when a mesh of ropes slammed into her, and she found herself caught and dangling in what was essentially a giant butterfly net.

Startled into submission, Witch-Hazel froze like a statue as the net drew her down and then into a giant basket hanging beneath the balloon. Through the interwoven ropes of the net draped over her face, she made out a rotund figure staring seriously at her over a wide nose and buck teeth. The figure was backlit by a small but roaring fire making her facial features hard to read, but she was wearing a pretty yellow sundress and was a dead-ringer for Twiggy.

"Witch-Hazel?" the beaver asked. "Is that actually you?"

"Twiggy!" Witch-Hazel exclaimed. She dropped hold of the book, which was tangled in the net with her, and tried to reach out to embrace the grumpy looking beaver. But the mesh of ropes got in her way.

"Let's get you untangled," Twiggy said with a sigh that whistled between her big front teeth.

"No, wait," Witch-Hazel objected. "There's an eagle … it'll probably chase after me. Can this balloon get us away from it?"

Another whistling sigh. "Of course," Twiggy said. "You always were good at making enemies." The beaver pulled a cord hanging down from the cloth balloon above them, and the tiny fire grew larger, roaring louder. And the beanstalk rushed past them downwards, or really, the balloon sprang upward.

"What is this thing we're in?" Witch-Hazel asked.

"A hot air balloon," Twiggy answered, pride creeping into her rumbly voice. "I invented it, so I could fly up to the All-Being and rescue Fish-Breath. I assume you're on the same quest." She didn't add any recriminations about the ineffectiveness of Witch-Hazel's travel strategies. She didn't have to. They hung in the air between beaver and squirrel anyway. Unsaid, but impossible to ignore.

Between the two travelers, one of them had a hot air balloon to travel by, stocked with baskets of provisions it would seem; Witch-Hazel saw the small baskets stacked in the corner, overflowing with dried fish jerky, fresh fruit, and roasted nuts. The smell of the food filled the larger basket they were both inside with a homey, safe feeling.

The other of the two travelers … had been falling from an angry eagle's nest, trying to use an old book as a parachute. And was now, most likely, being chased by that eagle.

There was nothing quite like Twiggy's hyper-competence to make Witch-Hazel feel foolish and useless.

Once the hot air balloon was well on its way, Twiggy let go of the cord that made the fire roar bigger. The flame dwindled down to its original size, and the beaver knelt over the tangle of mesh, squirrel, and book. Witch-Hazel had been hopelessly tangled in the rope as far as she could tell, yet Twiggy only had to twist the long handle attached to the net a few times to free her.

Abashed, Witch-Hazel gathered the spell book up, smoothing its pages. The tome was still open to the spell for Clear Eyes. And then she looked steadily at Twiggy and said, "Thank you."

Twiggy tried to brush her gratitude aside, but Witch-Hazel grabbed the beaver's big paws with her smaller ones.

"No, really. *Thank you.* I would have died if you weren't here."

Twiggy looked discomfited. She couldn't make eye contact with Witch-Hazel and, though she opened her mouth to speak, seemed unable to find any words to say. Before the pause between them could grow too awkward, a racket of chittering, chattering, and squawking interrupted them from above.

The ravens. Waiting to collect the book.

Witch-Hazel hadn't had time to read the spell for Clear Eyes, let alone learn it well enough to remember it. She was tempted to tear the page out, but she didn't want the ravens following her, harassing her, casting horrible fire and ice spells at her all the way up to the All-Being's castle as retribution. Better to hand the book over unaltered and count it as a missed opportunity.

Then a shriek from below changed everything in her reckoning. Witch-Hazel stood up and peered over the edge of the giant basket. The giant golden eagle was soaring after them, screaming revenge and murder.

Glancing upward, Witch-Hazel saw the smaller black ravens, circling, swooping, and fluttering about like autumn leaves on the wind.

"Can they pop your balloon?" Witch-Hazel asked nervously.

"With beaks and talons like that?" Twiggy pointed down at the eagle. "I'm sure they could!"

Witch-Hazel sized the situation up: there were a bunch of birds above and a big angry bird below. She needed them to focus on each other and lose interest in her. So, she gathered the book in her paws—it was what they all really wanted—and tore out the page for Clear Eyes. She folded up the torn page and tucked it into a hidden side pocket of her backpack. None of the birds would have time to check if the book was in perfect condition before they finished fighting with each other for it. Not if Witch-Hazel had her way.

The squirrel, quaking with fear, stood up and held the book high over her head, where the birds above and below could hopefully see it. She called out, loud as she could, "I played my part! I got the book! Now fight over it between yourselves, and leave me out of it!"

With all of her strength, she hurled the book away from the hot air balloon, away from the beanstalk, just away. It arced outward, curving to downward, fluttering and flapping like a dying bird. All the ravens above and the eagle below changed course, following the cursed spell book down.

Witch-Hazel turned to Twiggy and said, urgently, "Can this thing fly any faster?" With a twinge, she wondered if they'd already flown past Zwi and Mercy, waiting for her. Had they seen the balloon? Did they guess she was inside? Would they follow her? She couldn't stop and look for them … The balloon was too big, too colorful, too obvious, and they needed to get it out of the birds' sight before they stopped fighting each other for the book and decided to come after her for revenge.

Maybe they'd all kill each other, and she wouldn't have to worry about them.

Sometimes she worried about herself—that she'd become someone who could hope an entire colony of ravens and a mother eagle would all meet mutually murderous ends, just so she wouldn't have to fear them anymore. Had she become a monster? Could a squirrel become a monster, just for trying to save her own fluffy tail? Maybe.

She'd let Fish-Breath decide. Let him be her moral compass.

Or maybe … Twiggy. Could the beaver forgive her? Now that they were back together, traveling the same direction, pursuing the same quest?

The beaver was holding the cord that made the fire roar again, and the fire had flared into a blazing blue, yellow, and orange flame. The hot air balloon was plummeting upward, as if gravity had reversed for it and it alone.

Maybe Witch-Hazel wouldn't have to climb any farther. They could float the rest of the way to the All-Being's castle. Twiggy was so clever. It would have saved so much time and effort if the beaver had simply let Witch-Hazel continue traveling with her to begin with … but then, she wouldn't have met Mercy.

"I don't suppose you've seen a honeybee and a yellow—" The stars all around them reminded Witch-Hazel that they were deep into the night. "—I mean, green moth? They were supposed to be waiting for me, above the eagle's nest."

"Honeybee?" Twiggy asked, letting go of the rip cord. The fire died down to the size of a candle's flame—steady but small. "Are you and Zwi still traveling together? I never did trust that bee."

"I'm the one who lied to you, not her," Witch-Hazel blurted out impulsively. Defending Zwi might not be the best move for convincing Twiggy to forgive her. But it was right and fair. The correct thing to do. Besides, Zwi deserved Witch-Hazel's loyalty so much more than Twiggy did. The honeybee had stayed by her side when she'd needed someone, given her purpose and companionship.

Twiggy had abandoned her, making Witch-Hazel feel like everything had been her fault. But it hadn't been her fault that Twiggy and Fish-Breath were deep underground on a quest of their own, and it hadn't been her fault that a maniacal snake necromancer tried—and very nearly succeeded—to kill them.

Maybe Witch-Hazel didn't need Twiggy's forgiveness, or her friendship. Maybe she needed to go back to traveling alone. Or rather, climbing the beanstalk, ideally with Zwi and Mercy by her side. As soon as she could find them.

Witch-Hazel looked over the basket's edge, trying to gauge how hard it would be to jump back to the beanstalk. If Twiggy steered the balloon a little closer, she could jump quite easily. If not … she'd get there, but she'd fall a ways first.

"Sit down," Twiggy said gruffly. "You look a wreck. Have you eaten anything recently?"

"Beans," Witch-Hazel said. "So many beans."

Twiggy laughed, her teeth whistling. "You didn't pack anything else? You've just been eating what you can find on this beanstalk as you can climb?"

Witch-Hazel didn't know how to answer, but the smell of toasted nuts and fresh fruits was suddenly overpowering. She sat down and curled her tail around herself like a blanket. The clear night was cold and windy, and the balloon's rapid ascent made the wind chill even worse. She took off her backpack and pulled out the blue coat her mother had made for her. She put it on, and then she pulled the folded page with the spell for Clear Eyes out too. She didn't think she could read it in the limited light from the moon and small fire propelling the balloon, but she thought it would make herself feel better to hold it.

Twiggy filled a small wooden bowl with cherries and honey roasted almonds. Witch-Hazel's mouth was already watering by the time she took the offered bowl in her paws. The cherries and almonds tasted as good as any of the imaginary feasts she'd eaten in the unicorn's grove.

A terrible thought made Witch-Hazel's blood run cold, even with her warm coat on and tail wrapped around herself. She unfolded the spell for Clear Eyes and, almost reluctantly, peered through the darkness at the ancient lettering on the page. She needed to cast the spell, because she needed to know that Twiggy and this bizarre, magical, *extremely convenient* hot air balloon were real. They were too perfect to be real. Twiggy had appeared on a balloon, exactly when Witch-Hazel needed her to. That couldn't be real.

But the spell for Clear Eyes began with a long list of ingredients—juniper berries collected under full moonlight, a mushroom cap the exact shade of pink of a cherry blossom, yellow rose petals, silver salmon scales, teardrops from a broken heart … The list went on and on. Witch-Hazel had none of them, could collect none of them. Worse, even if she had time to collect all the arcane ingredients listed at the top of the spell, when she'd torn the page out of the book, a chunk from the middle of the page hadn't come. It must have stayed stuck in the spine, leaving the page in her hands looking like it'd had a big bite taken out of it, obscuring the instructions for what to do with all of the ingredients.

But …

At the bottom, the spell said, "Yn truthe, none yf these yngredients nor ynstructions be necessary. Hold thyne heart's truest hope closely, and thy eyes wyll see clear."

Witch-Hazel crumpled up the paper and threw it over the side of the basket. Let it fall to the birds below. Let them fight over it.

Magic was nonsense. All of it.

Witch-Hazel ate the rest of her bowl of cherries and almonds in bitter silence, but as she did, Twiggy pulled a blanket out from a hamper of supplies, beside the baskets of food. The beaver draped the blanket over the shivering squirrel and sat down beside her.

Witch-Hazel clung to her silence, but Twiggy—generally stoic, grumpy, and more interested in puzzles than talking—began to talk. She'd been traveling alone for the entire time that Witch-Hazel had traveled with Zwi.

Twiggy was lonely, and she couldn't resist the opportunity to pour out her heart to an old friend, even an old friend who she felt betrayed by and had wanted to never see again.

So, Witch-Hazel cuddled close to Twiggy, sharing warmth under the blanket, and listened to her tale of returning to Riverton where everything had seemed gray and pointless without Fish-Breath; consulting all the experts she could find; and finally, building herself a hot air balloon, which she then rode through the sky, traveling from one empty cloud to another, until finally one morning, she saw the beanstalk in the distance.

In return, Witch-Hazel told her own tale of traveling with Zwi, and she stopped worrying that Twiggy and the hot air balloon couldn't be real. Because if they weren't real, nothing was. Perhaps Witch-Hazel could imagine an improbable fox wedding, inspired by her owns dreams and desires, but she'd never imagined the idea of flying through the sky under the power of heated air, captured inside a balloon. She wasn't that clever. She didn't need to be. She was content with being able to recognize the magic of Twiggy's science without being able to discover it for herself.

The two friends, reunited, continued floating upward through the night.

17

As the sky brightened with pre-dawn light, Witch-Hazel shivered and realized she'd been sleeping. Twiggy was still asleep, and they were still ascending beside the beanstalk. Nothing had changed, expect maybe the clouds looked closer when she gazed up past the balloon.

The balloon was a riot of colors now that there was enough light to see them—red and blue stripes, yellow polka dots, green stars, and purple squiggles. If Witch-Hazel had been designing a balloon like this one, she'd have chosen all blue, white, and gray fabric, hoping the muted tones would let the balloon hide among the clouds in the sky. A stealth balloon. This one looked more like an entire carnival had been rolled up into a ball.

But then, Witch-Hazel rarely wore clothes, except for simple, serviceable pieces—her backpack, her warm coat, or maybe a belt to hold a pair of swords. Whereas Twiggy always dressed in pretty sundresses, as bright yellow as the sun or pink as carnations. The hot air balloon was a perfect expression of the beaver's aesthetics and engineering ingenuity.

Witch-Hazel loved Twiggy for being so strange and different and brilliant, and she could hardly believe that the beaver seemed to have forgiven her. They were friends again. Or at least, they had seemed to be friends last night, and Twiggy was still leaned against her, using Witch-Hazel's silver cloud of a tail as a pillow. She occasionally chittered in her sleep, working her teeth as if she were gnawing on a phantom tree limb.

A buzz from outside the basket made Witch-Hazel realize why she had woken up. The buzzing came and went, changing in volume. Carefully, Witch-Hazel extracted her tail from under Twiggy's head and stood up to look over the edge of the basket.

"Zwi!" Witch-Hazel called softly.

The bee zigged and zagged erratically, clearly having trouble keeping up with the balloon.

"Slow down!" she buzzed. "I've been flying all night, and I can't keep up. I had to leave Mercy behind, resting. She doesn't fly as fast as I do. But if you slow down, or stop, I can go back for her."

"Yes, of course!" Witch-Hazel called back, but then she looked around the balloon and had no clue how to operate it. She'd seen Twiggy pulling the cord to make the fire burn stronger, and that had made the balloon race faster upward. But she didn't know how to slow it down.

Witch-Hazel didn't want to disturb Twiggy. Their returned friendship was so new, possibly fragile. But she owed Zwi and Mercy more loyalty than Twiggy. So reluctantly, she shook the beaver awake and explained the situation.

Twiggy yawned and pulled the cord that Witch-Hazel thought would make the fire roar. Instead, it opened a gap at the top of the balloon. Apparently, there were multiple cords, and Witch-Hazel had mixed them up.

"The gap lets hot air out," Twiggy explained. "That will slow us down. Are we safely past the birds?"

"I don't know," Witch-Hazel said. "I hope so."

The beaver and squirrel breakfasted on apple slices and walnuts. By the time they finished, the whole sky was pale yellow, ready and waiting for the sun to rise. Zwi and Mercy arrived at the balloon and perched on the edge of the giant basket, just as the first rays of sunlight broke over the distant horizon.

Mercy's lime green wings shimmered and transformed. For a moment, her wings seemed as colorful and complicated as the rainbow splashed and stretched over the cloth of the balloon, but it must have been a trick of the light or Witch-Hazel's tired eyes, because they settled down into their usual daytime colors, turning the same yellow and black as the fuzzy body of the bee beside her.

Twiggy blinked. "You weren't making up stories last night."

"Of course not," Witch-Hazel said, affronted. "Why would I make up a story about a were-moth?"

"Why would you lie about having collected all of the Celestial Fragments?" Twiggy countered.

Witch-Hazel didn't have a good answer for that. Fortunately, the question wasn't tinged with the same bitterness or weight that it would have been the night before, when they'd first been reunited and hadn't yet spent hours reacquainting themselves with each other.

There's a certain magic to the kind of conversation that happens during the middle of the night, winding and wending its way through every random topic that occurs to the participants. Not the ridiculous kind of magic that ravens store in silly old books or unicorns use to confuse visitors to their gardens—no, a simple, pure magic of two hearts connecting when the minds they belong to are too tired to put up walls and guard themselves like they would during the harsh light of day.

With the missing members of Witch-Hazel's troupe safely inside the hot air balloon's basket, they were able to speed up again. But first, Witch-Hazel jumped out, back to the beanstalk, where she gathered armfuls of flowers for the bee and butterfly to feast upon.

Then the four of them—squirrel, beaver, bee, and butterfly—floated upward at full speed. Twiggy wanted to hear every detail of the illusions they'd seen in the unicorn's grove and sounded almost regretful that she hadn't been traveling with them. She seemed to wish she'd had the chance to see a unicorn, even if it came with the cost of spending a month dancing through the unicorn's veils of illusions. Twiggy didn't seem to believe that was a cost, no matter how much Witch-Hazel insisted that it had been. It had left her uncertain of the truth of her own eyes and ears. Even touching something with her paw was no longer enough to prove it was real.

Mercy grew quiet once again, in the face of a new, unfamiliar companion. Though by the time night fell and she'd turned back to a moth—meaning she'd transformed in front of Twiggy's eyes twice—she began hazarding a few words here and there again, showing nearly as much interest in Twiggy's stories as Twiggy had shown in theirs.

Mercy had seen so little of the world, and much of it hadn't been real. Stories were the best, fastest way for her to learn more.

Witch-Hazel felt a strange sense of peace settle over her as they floated upward, but it was mixed with a fluttery nervousness. What if she'd come all this way, and when she saw Fish-Breath again, it turned out that she'd imagined the connection between them? Twiggy was coming for Fish-Breath anyway. Twiggy was doing a much better job of it, and had saved Witch-Hazel's own expedition.

Perhaps Witch-Hazel's journey was superfluous, and when they arrived, the All-Being would bless a tree for Zwi, stabilize Mercy's form, reunite Twiggy with her best friend … and then look at the squirrel who had accompanied them with puzzlement. "Why are you here?" the

All-Being would ask, and Witch-Hazel wouldn't have an answer. She'd grow tongue-tied and confused as the others looked at her, happy with their prizes, and pitying her for wasting her time on a quest that wasn't really for her.

Or worse ... what if Fish-Breath was thrilled to see her, and it turned out that she didn't really like him? What if the jolly, jovial nature she remembered turned out to be tiresome and irritating? What if his jokes weren't funny, and his cooking wasn't good ... and when she saw his face, her heart didn't light up?

What if he was better off in the clouds with the All-Being?

Witch-Hazel wrapped her arms around her silver tail and watched the clouds pass by, tuning out the stories Twiggy was telling Mercy about her life in Riverton, and trying to numb herself to all the possibilities for horrible failure.

The clouds were wispy and thin. Cirrus clouds streamed past them like the currents in an ocean. The wind had been speeding up as they ascended, and Twiggy kept having to interrupt her stories to adjust the cloth of the balloon, steering them in circles around the beanstalk. Dizzying, spinning circles.

Witch-Hazel blinked in surprise. "Those flowers," she said, pointing at the beanstalk and interrupting an anecdote about the restaurants in Riverton. "Those are the same flowers that we passed an hour ago."

"They can't be," Zwi said. "We've been ascending all that time."

"Look at the pattern," Witch-Hazel insisted. "Purple flowers in a big cluster, next to pink flowers trailing away like a tail ... I noticed it before, because it was so unusual."

"It is an unusually big cluster of purple flowers," Zwi admitted. "But maybe they just grow that way."

Witch-Hazel shook her head, certain of what she'd seen.

Twiggy fiddled with the ropes hanging down from the rainbow balloon above them. Then she said, sounding very disappointed, "I think Witch-Hazel is right. My balloon can't fly any higher than this, and at this point, we're just letting the winds toss us about. We have to get out and climb."

"Why can't it fly higher?" Witch-Hazel asked.

"Haven't you noticed the air growing thinner?" Twiggy gasped a little between words, and Witch-Hazel realized she'd been breathing shallowly too. "The balloon relies upon the hot air being thinner than the air around it, but the air up here ..." The beaver shuddered, glanced upward, and then sighed deeply. "I don't know if I can make it. I get out of breath easily at the best of times."

"What was your plan for final leg of the journey?" Witch-Hazel asked. "The part that called for the Endless Breath granted by the Moon Opal?"

Twiggy shrugged. "I had hoped the legends were wrong, and the part about needing the Endless Breath of a fish were more poetic license than accurate fact."

Witch-Hazel couldn't help feeling a glow of pride: she had planned for this part of the journey. In fact, Fish-Breath had provided the plan, when he sent her a vision under the lake during the forest fire. Witch-Hazel opened her backpack and pulled out the air lily she'd braided into a necklace. She held it out to Twiggy, and when the beaver looked uncertain, placed it over the beaver's head herself.

As soon as the geometrical white flower—dried and crinkly but still pretty—settled on Twiggy's breast, just above the neckline of her sundress, the beaver drew a deep breath and then laughed. "That's amazing."

"Air lilies," Witch-Hazel said distractedly, already focused on braiding one of the extras into a second garland for herself. It was a little trickier now that they were dried, but she managed and placed the garland over her own head. She'd already begun breathing easier, as soon as she touched them. She was so glad she'd brought along a bag full of extras, so there were enough to share with Twiggy. "I'd make garlands for you two as well," she said to the two insects watching, "but I don't think you're big enough to wear them."

In answer, Mercy fluttered over and landed on the dried flower resting near Witch-Hazel's heart. Zwi flew over to the air lily worn around Twiggy's neck and landed there.

"This will do," Zwi buzzed. "You'll have to carry us."

"Fortunately, we're light," Mercy said.

"I'm not built for climbing …" Twiggy looked nervously at the beanstalk and then glanced back at her baskets of supplies. They'd have to be left behind. The beaver clearly didn't want to leave her cozy hot air balloon basket, but if the balloon could rise no higher, there was no choice.

18

TWIGGY INSISTED ON stuffing the bottom of Witch-Hazel's backpack full of dried nuts and fruit, leaving enough room in the top for the extra air lilies, and then the beaver settled a similarly full backpack on her own back, before cautiously following Witch-Hazel out of the hot air balloon's basket and onto the twining vines of the beanstalk. She carefully anchored the balloon to the beanstalk with ropes, so it would be waiting for them when they returned.

If they returned from the All-Being's castle.

And if they returned by the same path they'd taken to get there.

As Twiggy had said, she wasn't built for climbing, and Witch-Hazel had to move frustratingly slowly to keep from leaving her behind.

They were so close.

Witch-Hazel could see the clouds gathered into an impenetrable white gauze above them. If she could only dash up the vine by herself, she could be there in no time. But she had to wait for Twiggy.

The beaver's claws were wrong—too dull for clinging, like shovels not grappling hooks. Her tail was wrong too—broad and flat, throwing her off balance instead of aiding her. And her whole body, strong and powerful, was a liability—the extra weight slowing her down and dragging her down.

Whereas Witch-Hazel's lithe, willowy form—much less useful for whacking zombies out of her way—was perfect here. Agile, quick, and claws sharp as needles for digging into plant flesh.

Still, they kept climbing, and the clouds above grew closer and closer. Witch-Hazel couldn't pinpoint when it had happened, but eventually, she looked around and realized the cottony white completely surrounded them. She couldn't see the ground anymore, nor any sky above. Nothing in the distance. Only the wooly whiteness of the clouds.

"Shouldn't the sun have set by now?" Witch-Hazel asked.

Grunting and breathless, in spite of the air lily around her neck, Twiggy answered, "How can you tell it hasn't with all these clouds?"

"It's not dark."

"Could be moon glow," Twiggy said. "It's dim enough."

"But ..." Witch-Hazel stared at Mercy's wings—the perfect barometer for whether it was daytime or night—flapping slowly on the flower resting on her chest.

Witch-Hazel hadn't noticed Mercy changing ... her wings hadn't shimmered like usual, and they hadn't returned to the pale lime green shade of her moth form. But they weren't yellow-and-black tiger swallowtail wings either. They'd grown patchy—mostly yellow, black, and pale green, but they also had gemlike touches of red, blue, and magenta. More than anything, they now made Witch-Hazel think of the carnival colors of Twiggy's rainbow balloon. "What's happening to you, Mercy? Do you know?"

"I think … I'm remembering who I really am." The rainbow butterfly's words sounded musical, like she was singing the melody of a dimly remembered song, making up the words as she went, and hoping to stumble her way into finding the real lyrics.

Witch-Hazel stopped climbing, haunted by the emotions stirred in her breast by Mercy's voice—intense longing and gentle contentment, as if she were staring at a magical castle from a great distance, soaking up the beauty while imagining what her life would be like if she lived there: a royal resident roaming the gardens and grounds, dressed in silks and satins, and sighing for the freedom of being a simple squirrel in a grove of oak trees.

But then she realized: she was staring at a castle. The clouds had parted, and the golden towers, turrets, and spires gleamed as bright and shining as the sun. The castle was surrounded by gardens—pearlescent shrubberies, pruned into clever mazes; ivory trees with leaves as lively and bright as falling snow; and row upon row of rose bushes bursting with flowers as pure and dazzling as sunlight on water.

She turned away, but when she risked looking back, the castle was still there. As real as the beanstalk beneath her claws; as real as Carnelian's wedding.

Witch-Hazel no longer trusted her eyes, but she trusted her friends. "Do you see it? Is the castle really there?" She turned to watch Twiggy's expression, but the beaver didn't answer. She'd stopped climbing too and stared wordlessly at the sight above them, eyes twinkling with tears.

The sight was beautiful, but it hadn't made Witch-Hazel feel like crying. Was there something wrong with her? Did the beauty not sink into her soul the way it did for Twiggy? Or had she imagined it? Was Twiggy crying, because she saw the truth: they'd climbed up here for nothing.

There was no castle in the clouds. They were fools.

Witch-Hazel had always been a fool.

She turned her face upward again, steeled to see a sky blank except for distant stars, now that they were past the clouds. But then she saw what had brought tears to Twiggy's eyes instead: Fish-Breath hovered in the clouds above them, tawny-feathered wings stretched out wide, flapping gently to keep him in the air.

It made no sense for an otter to have wings, yet as Witch-Hazel gazed at Fish-Breath, it was hard for her to imagine that any otter was ever built differently.

Fish-Breath looked perfectly natural with wings.

"Ho there!" he called, as jovial and perfect as ever, and Witch-Hazel's heart melted. Utterly melted.

"I don't suppose you could spare a pair of wings like that for me?" Twiggy called back, her voice breaking with emotion. "Climbing this overgrown weed is rather difficult for an old river rafter like me."

"Against the rules, I'm afraid," he called back, as cheerful as an otter swooping through the sky on feathered wings could be. Before they could say anything else to him, he flew back to the castle and disappeared inside its golden gates.

Twiggy grumbled, but she began climbing twice as fast. Her heart had caught a second wind at the sight of Fish-Breath.

Witch-Hazel began to fall behind, climbing cautiously, uncertain of what exactly she was climbing toward. What rules could Fish-Breath mean?

The vines of the beanstalk spread out, unraveling into a leafy canopy that dissipated into the cottony, wooly grounds of the cloudscape. Bits of green leaf stuck out of the cloud here and there, and thin vines curled along the fluffy ground. Twiggy was the first to test setting paw to cloud, and her paw held firm. A broad smile broke across her face. Well, as broad as could be, given her narrow mouth and large front teeth. "No more climbing!" she cried. "Hallelujah!"

Witch-Hazel reluctantly followed suit, fearful that her small paws would sink right through the soft surface where Twiggy's paws were saved from that fate by their aquatic webbing.

The surface of the cloud held firm. It felt like a snow drift—soft, giving, but slightly crunchy on the top in a very satisfying way—except warm like a smooth river rock, poking above the surface of the streaming water, that's been absorbing sunlight all afternoon. Witch-Hazel sighed in contentment. She was surrounded by beauty so deep that it soaked through her fur and skin to warm the bones below.

Yet, as much as she wanted to lie down on the cloud and stare at the pearly roses and ivory trees all around her forever, she couldn't forget Carnelian melting away into nothing but a shadow.

Was any of this real?

The rainbow butterfly resting on the air lily pendant strung around Witch-Hazel's neck flapped her wings and floated gently into the air. Zwi watched from where she was perched on Twiggy's lily pendant. Her antennae circled curiously. "We can breathe here without the lilies?"

"I can," the butterfly who had once been Mercy answered. Her wings reminded Witch-Hazel of the stained glass windows in the church at the end of the underground labyrinth. Beautiful, colorful, and somehow portending danger all around.

Zwi interpreted the butterfly's answer in the simplest possible way—the air was thick enough to breathe again—and took flight as well. She zigged and zagged between Twiggy and Witch-Hazel, seeming impatient for them to move toward the castle. So, apparently, she could breathe without the lily's help here too. Though, Witch-Hazel hadn't been at all sure of that.

Witch-Hazel suspected Mercy could do many things that mortals like herself, Twiggy, and Zwi couldn't. Because she recognized those wings now: Mercy was the butterfly from her vision in the underwater tree's amber looking glass. She was one of the four gods who'd consorted with the All-Being for all those years, dancing, holding feasts and balls, and finally arguing with each other as the endless rivers dried up and all the vines connecting the earth to the clouds had withered and died. All the vines except this one.

Twiggy continued toward the castle with both insects flying beside her, until she noticed that Witch-Hazel wasn't with them. She stopped, turned back, and asked, "Are you okay? We're almost there!"

"Haven't either of you noticed that Mercy's wings have changed?" Witch-Hazel asked. "Or is your name even Mercy anymore?"

Twiggy looked puzzled, and Zwi flew in a curlicue around Mercy. The butterfly hovered peacefully, unbothered by their examination and equally unbothered by Witch-Hazel's question. "I love the name you gave me," Mercy said in her sing-song voice. "I have no plans to change it."

"But your wings have changed," Witch-Hazel insisted.

"Her wings change every day," Zwi buzzed irritably. "You know that. If they're changing in a different way, perhaps it just means they're balancing out. That's why we brought her here, right? So, the All-Being could reunite you with Fish-Breath, bless a tree for my hive, and cure Mercy's afflicted state." She flew over to Witch-Hazel and landed on the air lily still resting on her breast. "Did you assume you knew how the All-Being would cure her? Presuming to know the mind of a god—"

"She's the butterfly from my vision," Witch-Hazel interrupted Zwi's admonition. "She's the Queen of the Air Realm. I recognize her."

Now Zwi did look startled. She buzzed softly, as if intending only Witch-Hazel to hear, "Are you sure?"

"She's the third queen of the elements I've met," Witch-Hazel said. There was an air of weight and power in each queen's presence. She could feel it like a cold breeze prickling the fur at the base of her ears. "I'm sure."

"We've been traveling with a queen of the elements ..." Zwi's buzz was a soft and reverential as a new

198

kitten's purr. "I've told her all the stories of my people, danced every dance I knew … so self-centered … What must she think of me?"

The butterfly floated closer on a breeze that smelled of distant apple blossoms and blackberry vines. "That you are kind, even when you are scared," she sang. "You cared for me, even when you feared it could cost you dearly."

Zwi lowered her antennae and crossed her first four legs in a pious bow. "My lady, my queen," she buzzed.

"There is no need for that," Mercy said, fluttering in the breeze like cherry blossoms in spring. "We are friends, are we not?"

"My lowness would not presume to friendship with the highness of a queen …" Zwi did not raise her head; if her eyes had been shaped differently—not faceted so she could see in every direction at once—she clearly would have averted them, afraid to dirty a queen of queens with her worker's gaze.

"There is no presumption," Mercy said. She landed on the dried air lily as well and lifted a graceful magenta talon toward Zwi. Her body had stayed the fuzzy white of a Luna moth, but grown as slender as the tiger-striped body of a swallowtail.

Reluctantly, Zwi reached one of her own obsidian talons out to take hold of Mercy's. They stood on the dried flower, on Witch-Hazel's chest, talon in talon, until Zwi relented and lifted her head to gaze at the butterfly goddess who she'd raised from an egg, through caterpillar days, back to her godhood.

"Come to the castle," Mercy said. "Our journey together is nearly done, and while I wish it could last longer, I'm also eager to return home. I've been away so long ..." The wispy flute solo of her voice sang of multitudes of years—lifetimes of years—in its sweet but melancholy tone. She sounded older than the oldest squirrel Witch-Hazel had ever met; older than the trees they lived in; older than the stones in the ground. And if she was a god—Queen of the Air Realm—then she most likely was older than anything else Witch-Hazel knew.

All three of the travelers—squirrel, beaver, and bee—couldn't help but obey her. They walked silently through the beautiful grounds toward the entrance to the shining castle.

19

MERCY FLOATED LIKE a dream, as colorful and ethereal as a soap bubble. But the snow-like cloud crunched under Witch-Hazel's paws in a very grounding way. She'd had dreams where she felt absolutely, completely certain that she was awake. And yet, it was the certainty of a player on the stage of dreamland. This was reality. She didn't have to feel certain or uncertain of the reality, no matter how strange it was. It simply was.

She walked through the castle's golden gates and saw the golden throne from the amber vision ahead of her. A figure sat on the throne, a complicated conglomeration of parts—a lion's haunches on one side, paired with a zebra's leg on the other; the forelegs of a bear and a deer; and a pair of arms as well, one monkey and one raccoon. Sprouting from the creature's back were a plethora of wings—one like the eagle's, another like the ravens', but also a rich, orange monarch butterfly wing and a lacy, translucent dragonfly wing. A bat wing. A wing that might have been a dragon's, if dragons were real.

When Witch-Hazel had pictured the All-Being, she'd known to picture a creature composed of all the best parts of every creature, but somehow, she'd only ever imagined two eyes. Yet, the All-Being's face puckered with eyes of every shape, color, and size—brown and soft, blue and bright, gold and gleaming, silver and coolly calculating. Her eyes made the multifaceted eyes on Zwi's and Mercy's faces seem simple. Witch-Hazel saw no spider parts specifically in the mix, but the effect overall made her think of a spider—too many limbs, too many eyes, but somehow, also exactly the right number.

Witch-Hazel had begun her quest under the earth, because she wanted to meet the All-Being. She wanted to look the deity in her eyes and see herself reflected there. She'd been sure that the All-Being would have a tail like hers—silver and flowing like a waterfall. And though many tails twitched behind the All-Being—scaly and sinuous, fuzzy and tufted, flowing like a horse's tail—none of them were like a squirrel's.

The All-Being stepped down from her throne—zebra hoof clopping against the glossy golden floor, and lion claws clicking. With each step, her limbs, wings, and tails shimmered like Mercy's wings had at dawn and dusk. She changed forms, seamlessly flowing from one shape into the next.

How did she know how to move when her body was constantly changing? And yet she moved with the grace of a deer in a forest, a salmon slipping through river currents, or a winged otter flying through the sky.

"Where is Fish-Breath?" Witch-Hazel called out, trying not to let the approaching goddess intimidate her. "We've come for our friend. He was just outside, greeting us. Where'd he go?"

The All-Being continued toward them without the slightest acknowledgment of Witch-Hazel's words, and the squirrel felt stung. Not only did she not see herself reflected in her goddesses' form—a form that flickered through the entirety of creation—she couldn't even inspire the goddesses' attention while standing right in front of her.

The All-Being stopped, a few paces in front of them, close enough to make Witch-Hazel's heart pound in fear from all the predator eyes that could see her and all the predator claws that could reach her. The All-Being held out a paw, and Mercy floated down like a soap bubble from above. The rainbow butterfly landed delicately on her outstretched paw, silky and black as midnight. A cat's paw. Yet as soon as Mercy landed, the paw shimmered, changing to a crooked bird's talon, bronze and rough.

Witch-Hazel remembered dreams where she'd insisted she'd been awake, arguing with everyone around her, certain she could prove the dream was reality.

She wished that option were open to her now. She wished that she had to *argue* and *insist* to prove this was reality, because it was so strange and dreamlike that it shouldn't have been real.

Beneath her breath, Witch-Hazel began chanting the words from the bottom of the spell for Clear Eyes to herself like a mantra: "*Hold thy heart's truest hope closely, and thy eyes will see clear.*" She didn't believe the spell would work, and she wasn't sure what it meant. But it couldn't hurt, and it gave her something solid to cling to. The words echoed in her head with a finality in their repetition that left no space for panicking.

"Where did you hear those words?" the All-Being asked, finally noticing the squirrel and fixing her with a many-eyed gaze.

The startlement of suddenly being noticed, when she didn't expect it and no longer wanted to be, sparked electrically along Witch-Hazel's spine. "What words?" she asked, not so much feigning ignorance as simply not believing a deity could care about what she had been chanting under her breath to calm herself.

The All-Being continued to stare with changing eyes, but she said nothing more.

Finally, Witch-Hazel said, "I read them in a spell book that belonged to the ravens, a day's climb beneath your castle."

"Ah, the ravens. They sneak into my library and copy down spells often. But that one … Why that one … Do you think this is an illusion?" the All-Being asked, settling on a mismatched pair of haunches—covered in wooly, bushy fur like a buffalo on one side and delicately, downy fur on the other, much like a mouse: a massive hoof paired with a tiny hand-like paw. Somehow, the inconsistency in size wasn't a problem, though, as if the shape of space itself distorted around the All-Being to make her flickering form make physical sense. "Do you think I'm an illusion?"

When faced with a god, honesty is the best policy. At least, that was Witch-Hazel's guess. "I don't know," she said. "I don't trust my eyes or ears anymore, not after everything I've been through. And you're unlike anything I've ever known."

The All-Being's voice sounded like a chorus singing as she replied, "Some would say that I am like *everything* you've ever known."

Witch-Hazel shook her head, and looked down at her paws, conveniently averting her gaze from the overwhelming, troubling nature of the deity before her. "They've never seen you," she muttered. "I can tell that now. Or they wouldn't tell the stories they do."

Gently, a paw touched Witch-Hazel's chin, and lifted her face to look at the All-Being again. But this time, Witch-Hazel could have been looking in a mirror. Bright brown eyes—a single pair—looked back at her from beneath perky, pointy ears; short, gray fur with tawny brown highlights faded to white on the All-Being's belly; and her crowning glory was a tail that curled over and cascaded like a silver waterfall.

Witch-Hazel reached up a paw and took hold of the All-Being's paw, still resting on the side of her face. She knew her eyes sparkled with joy at the sight of herself reflected in her god, because she saw the god's eyes sparkle back at her.

Witch-Hazel grabbed the All-Being's hand tightly with both paws. She squeezed. She didn't know what to do with all the joy she felt at seeing herself—her clumsy, confused, lost self—reflected so completely in the perfection of her world's god. She wanted to hold the joy close, save it up, store it for later, or maybe just live in that moment forever.

She felt grateful, so much gratitude, but she couldn't find any words to express it. She didn't know what to say, so she just stared, soaking up the love and completeness of seeing how she too could embody the divine.

Eventually, the moment ended, and the All-Being traded one squirrel's paw for an otter's webbed one; the other arm shimmered and morphed into a mallard's brown-speckled wing. She grew a giraffe's leg, an elephant's flappy ear, and sprouted all different kinds of tails in place of the perfect squirrel tail.

Witch-Hazel backed away. She couldn't help the fluttery fear she felt inside at the sight of hooves large enough to crush her; maws large enough to swallow her whole; and eyes that stared at her with a hawk's cool, appraising stare, ready to swoop down and destroy whatever they had fixed upon.

Yet, she knew that she was inside there too, now. Mixed in with all the other creatures, there was also the nature of a squirrel. A small, skittery animal, designed to spend her life searching for shiny chestnuts, hiding them in treasure troves buried under a tree's root, and then looking for them, hopelessly, again and again. She didn't know why she'd been made the way she had been, but she knew it was right. She was exactly who she was meant to be. Even if she didn't understand it.

"There are no illusions here," the All-Being said from mouths and muzzles of all shapes and sizes, changing and moving in her bizarre yet perfect face. "Sometimes, though, I wish there were."

Mercy, who had been floating beside the All-Being, landed on an outstretched paw of hers again.

"What did you learn during your years among the mortals, Queen Mercy?" the All-Being asked the rainbow butterfly resting on her changing paw.

"You know my new name," Mercy said.

The All-Being shrugged, a complicated but beautiful gesture. "From the fact that you've chosen to keep it, I can guess a little about the lesson you've taken from your journey into mortality."

"I've lived as nearly every kind of insect, and a few birds," Mercy said. "I tried to come back to you for many years in my butterfly form, but a sisterhood of butterflies took it upon themselves to stop my return, destroying every egg I could possibly have hatched from."

The fur at the base of Witch-Hazel's neck prickled, and she mouthed the words, but didn't give breath to them: "Every egg laid at the exact moment of dawn." Her choice at that fairy ring had been instrumental in saving the life of a god. She didn't know how to feel about that.

"The squirrel saved me," Mercy said, gesturing at her with a long graceful leg. "The bee educated me with her dances. The beaver rescued us with her ingenuity."

"Yes, I saw the hot air balloon," the All-Being agreed. "Quite ingenious. It makes one wonder whether the world needs magic after all. Science seems quite sufficient."

Twiggy cleared her throat and said, awkwardly, "Actually, oh great one, it wasn't. My balloon got us away from the birds chasing my friends, but we couldn't have made it here without these magic flowers." She held up the dried air lily on its garland around her neck, before letting it settle back on her chest, just above the fancy ruffles of her sundress.

Boldly, Witch-Hazel added, "And I would never have found the flowers, if our friend Fish-Breath hadn't sent me a vision of himself, guiding me to where they grow."

The All-Being waved a shimmering paw dismissively—the gesture began with gray fur on slender fingers and ended with green scales ending in blunted claws. "You need magic to reach magic. If we let the castle crumble and magic drain from the world, there will be no more call for it in the first place."

"What?" cried Twiggy, sounding a great deal like the squawking of a badly misused oboe. "I've come all this way to offer my services as an engineer—to help fix the great engines and turbines that make the endless rivers flow between the earth and the sky—and instead, you're planning on severing the connection completely?"

Witch-Hazel had never heard the beaver sound so angry. Her tirade echoed through the golden hall of the castle throne room. Personally, Witch-Hazel wasn't sure that a world without magic sounded so bad. No ghost moles. No sorcerer crabs. No zombie reptiles. And no unicorn gardens filled with pretty lies.

There would still be wind rustling through leaves on a summer day. Cool streams and warm river rocks. Sugared nuts and fresh strawberries. Friendships with bees, beavers, and otters.

"Where's Fish-Breath?" Witch-Hazel repeated, hoping this time to have her question heard and answered.

The hush that followed curdled coldly in Witch-Hazel's stomach. She worried that after coming all this way, Fish-Breath wasn't really here. Maybe, he'd died after all, in that battle beneath the earth, murdered by zombies, and the visions she'd had were visitations from an angel. Or maybe, the All-Being had saved him and brought him here, but he'd fallen into a deep, enchanted sleep—trapped in his unconscious, and sending out visions of himself through dreams.

But since the All-Being insisted there were no illusions here—no angels, no dreams—all they'd find was a cold body, sleeping or dead.

The mind is a wondrous tool, capable of spinning fears so fast that they fit in the moments between a question and an answer.

The All-Being spoke with her choir-like voice: "The otter has been working tirelessly since he arrived here, trying to fix the turbines that made the waters of the looping rivers flow. But they aren't broken. I've told him that, but he simply mutters something about needing more twigs and keeps puttering. I don't know what he thinks he needs twigs for."

"Twiggy," Witch-Hazel corrected. "He must be saying that he needs Twiggy." She glanced over her shoulder at the beaver, still standing a step behind her, and smiled; Twiggy smiled back, uncertainly. "What's wrong?" Witch-Hazel asked. "He's waiting for you! *Wanting* you." Witch-Hazel felt a spike of jealousy flare, heating her ears. She didn't know if Fish-Breath was waiting for her … yet, he'd sent her the underwater vision. He must have wanted her to come as well. Or maybe, he'd thought she was still traveling with Twiggy, and helping her would bring the beaver engineer, his best friend, to him sooner.

"If the turbines aren't broken …" Twiggy began, saying each word carefully, as if they were river rocks and she was stepping on them, one paw at at time, trying to traverse the rapid waters without falling in.

The All-Being waved a paw that shimmered and transformed into a wing, sweeping through the air, conjuring a white mist trailing behind it. The mist condensed, coalescing into a cloudy shape. A small figure appeared. From some angles, the cloudy figure looked like an animal, perhaps a small mammal or maybe the shape of a songbird … but like the All-Being herself, its shape seemed flickering and uncertain. Perhaps, Witch-Hazel only imagined the small cloud to have an animal's shape, the same way that one might find familiar shapes in the clouds floating across a summer sky.

"My Nimbus Elf will show you the way," the All-Being said, and the cloudy figure shuffled, seeming to bow and prance, heading away toward a corridor that lead out of the left side of the throne room.

Witch-Hazel and Twiggy exchanged a glance; the squirrel was sure she looked just as surprised at the sight of the Nimbus Elf as the beaver did. But then Twiggy scurried, waddling as fast as she could after the prancing cloud figure. Witch-Hazel hesitated, looking to Zwi before leaving. But the bee buzzed, "Go, find your friend. I'll be here when you return …"

She didn't have to say that she intended to stay behind and ask the All-Being about blessing a tree for her. She'd sacrificed so much to find her hive a new home. "Good luck," Witch-Hazel said, then she scurried away after the Nimbus Elf as well.

20

THE THRONE ROOM at the entrance to the castle had been tall, wide, and lined with decorative columns. Spacious and intimidating. Everything gold, as if they'd walked into the interior of the sun. The corridor leading away from it was impressive too, but the style was different.

Instead of broad expanses of gold, the hallway was lined with complicated tile patterns—mostly gold, but with detail work in all different colors, coming together in beautiful spirals and patterns. The floor was lined with carpets beautiful enough to be tapestries decorating the walls. Witch-Hazel felt almost wrong walking along them, worrying that her claws might snag the intricate stitching and leave a permanent mark, showing a clumsy squirrel had been here.

Witch-Hazel stopped briefly at a wide window and looked down to see the castle grounds from a different angle. Now that she knew about the Nimbus Elves, she saw them cavorting and capering all through the grounds—trimming the pearlescent hedges, tending the ivory trees, and collecting flowers from the shining white rose bushes. They'd been easy to miss before—they looked like pieces of cloud broken off from the larger clouds below, like a tuft of cotton candy that you pull off the paper cone, bite-sized and ready to pop in your mouth.

Were they creatures? Did they live in all the clouds? Or did the All-Being create them somehow? It had looked like the All-Being was creating a spirit out of air and water when she waved her wing, but now Witch-Hazel thought she'd merely been summoning one—a creature who already existed—to her side.

Reluctantly, Witch-Hazel moved away from the impressive, panoramic view. She thought she could stare at that view forever. But ... Fish-Breath was waiting.

Or perhaps, that was why Witch-Hazel wanted to keep staring out the window. She was afraid. Afraid of seeing Fish-Breath, for real, instead of as a vision or from a distance, and having the moment be ... disappointing. Not worth the journey. Afraid that she might be superfluous.

At the end of the window-lined corridor, the Nimbus Elf turned and went through a golden door. Twiggy followed. When Witch-Hazel caught up with them, she hesitated. But she'd come this far. She stepped through the door.

The throne room had seemed large, but this room dwarfed it. Most of the castle must have been contained within this one gigantic room, and the room was filled with cogs and gears, pistons and conveyers, mechanical intricacies that defied Witch-Hazel's imagination. Everything ca-thunked and whirr-ch-ch-chinged. The look on Twiggy's face showed that the beaver thought she had stepped into heaven. The literal, physical embodiment of heaven.

The Nimbus Elf leapt along a passageway between two towering wheels, turning on their axels, and lifting empty buckets toward the distant ceiling, then bringing them back down as they rattled and clanked. Reluctantly, Witch-Hazel followed.

Witch-Hazel was reluctant, because she didn't like being so near such complicated machinery. What if it broke down? She curled her tail closely around herself, afraid of catching it in any of the turning gears or moving widgets. Twiggy followed reluctantly as well, but her reluctance clearly stemmed from a different source: she wanted to stop and examine every piece of the giant turbine that filled the castle.

In the very heart of the engine, the Nimbus Elf brought them to Fish-Breath. The otter held a paw raised, pointing at the buckets and counting them as they turned on the giant wheel. He seemed to be muttering under his breath, and his wings—his improbably, beautiful, tawny-feathered wings—were folded tightly against his back. A diamond glittered on his wrist—no, not a diamond. The Star Sliver. The silver circlet that the sparkling fragment had been set in had vanished, but the twinkling gem itself seemed to have sunk into his fur, right where a human might have worn a gleaming watch face, and become part of him.

Twiggy rushed forward, and the otter and beaver immediately fell into their old rapport, exclamations of delight at seeing each other transitioning naturally into discussing the machinations of the turbine around them, a machine they had both so desperately wanted to see since before they'd ever met Witch-Hazel.

But Witch-Hazel held back, tilting her head, and searching Fish-Breath with her eyes to see if the other Celestial Treasures had become a part of him as well.

When he lifted his other paw, gesturing at a large, toothy gear in the machine, she saw the sleepy gleam of the Moon Opal, encrusted on the furry knuckle of his webbed paw, like a barnacle on a whale. And yes, on his breast, the Sun Shard glowed, throwing off bits of light like sparks from its topaz facets.

The ring the Moon Opal had been set in was gone, as was the golden chain the Sun Shard used to hang from. They had grown into Fish-Breath's skin, under his fur. He was more than an otter now—a celestial creature, granted wings, strength, and endless breath by the three gems.

Maybe he belonged here, up in the sky, in a castle filled with living clouds.

Still talking animatedly with Twiggy, Fish-Breath opened a panel in one of the machine's consoles, revealing rows of buttons, switches, and dials underneath. Twiggy's paws touched the controls reverently, passing over them as if she could read a story in their shapes. Another language Witch-Hazel didn't speak. She couldn't understand Zwi's dancing, nor Twiggy's communion with machines.

While the beaver was absorbed, Fish-Breath grew fidgety. He'd been here for months already, examining this machine as if it were a giant puzzle for him to solve, at least if the All-Being were to be believed. He glanced over and saw Witch-Hazel. When their eyes met, his muzzle split into the widest grin.

He rushed toward her, wings stretching out behind him, and wrapped his arms around the much smaller squirrel, barely half his height. He lifted her from the ground and swung her around in a tight hug. "Witch-Hazel! You came!"

Witch-Hazel wasn't sure, wrapped so tightly in his arms, but it seemed that his wings had lifted the two of them right off the floor. She'd expected her heart to fill with joy, nearly to the point of bursting, when they were together again, but instead, it felt like a tangled knot inside of her was loosening, all of the anxiety and fear and loss washing away, leaving only a sense of rightness and relief. She was with her otter again. She could have cried … except she didn't need to anymore. Finally. By the time he let go of her, stepping back to see her better, their hind paws were back on the floor. He held her front paws tightly with his own.

Her paws felt safe wrapped in the webbing of his paws, but she pulled her paws free, turned his right paw over, and ran her claw tips gently around the Moon Opal encrusted on his knuckle. Round, smooth, and dancing with ribbons of color whenever the light hit it.

"Yeah …" he said. "The Celestial Fragments kind of fused into me." He shrugged, laughed, and said, "I guess, if you want them back, you'll have to take the whole otter who's attached to them!" He rubbed at the Star Sliver gleaming on his wrist with his other paw.

"I don't think I'd mind that," Witch-Hazel said, shyly. Although, she worried that the All-Being wouldn't let the Celestial Fragments go, that they might be required to stay in her palace in the sky, trapping Fish-Breath here forever. "Though, I don't really care about the treasures anymore. They were just supposed to help me get here …" Now she shrugged, gesturing at the bizarre machine around them. "Well, I'm here."

"You *are,*" he said enthusiastically. "I'd love to show you around …"

Now he sounded shy, and that made Witch-Hazel smile. She nodded. "Please, show me everything." She didn't want to stay here, trapped in the castle in the sky, but she did want to see it.

Fish-Breath politely offered to bring Twiggy on the tour, but she waved him off, not even taking her eyes from the machine. She hadn't really come here for him. She'd come to solve the riddle of why the endless rivers had dried up and focus all her expertise on starting them again.

Witch-Hazel, however, had come for Fish-Breath.

The two of them—perfectly normal squirrel and celestially enhanced otter—strolled through halls of the castle and then the gardens surrounding it. They literally walked along the clouds together, paw in paw, catching up and sharing stories. Fish-Breath laughed at all of Witch-Hazel's jokes and stared at her with absolute focus during the intense parts of her stories. He made her feel like the most fascinating and important creature who'd ever lived, even though the stories she was telling were filled with creatures she thought were much more interesting—Mercy, Gloaming, even the imaginary Carnelian and her betrothed Harvey. But then, Carnelian and Harvey had been aspects of Witch-Hazel's own imagination, so maybe they were a credit to her creativity after all.

Once Fish-Breath was caught up on the journey she'd taken to reunite them, he told her everything he'd learned about the castle, the Nimbus Elves, the All-Being, and the falling out that the three Queens and one King of the elements had, leading to the end of an era. The drying up of the rivers. The withering of the vines.

"The mouse king chipped the Celestial Fragments out of the Sun, Moon, and North Star." As Fish-Breath spoke of each Treasure, he touched it lightly with his free paw, a seemingly unconscious gesture. "He was jealous of how they sparkled and shined, unlike the Earth of his own realm and wanted to keep pieces of them for himself. But the cracks left behind … magic began leaking out of them. The All-Being insisted that the mouse king return the fragments and heal the cracks, but instead, he hid them and ran away. With the world out of balance due to the mouse king hiding, and magic draining away, the Queens of the Fire and Water Realms began fighting over territory …"

"The forest fires and deluges …" Witch-Hazel said with wonder, remembering how she'd felt like she could see straight into the salamander queen's Fire Realm in the flames. The gods had been fighting a war over the gemstones encrusting her beloved otter. They would want them back.

"Yes," Fish-Breath agreed. "As soon as you told your story, I was sure the fires and floods you'd seen were part of their war."

"The Queen of the Air Realm?" Witch-Hazel asked, hoping that Mercy at least would be on her side and wouldn't let the others take Fish-Breath away from her again. "Is she part of the war? If so, why was she an unhatched egg for us to find?"

"The Queen of the Air Realm was uncertain of what side to take. So, she decided to live among her people and try to discern whether magic was worth saving, or whether it was better to let the magic drain from the world after all."

"I wonder what she concluded ..." Witch-Hazel mused. She also wondered how her own prejudices and preferences—not to mention Zwi's—might have affected the royal butterfly's conclusions. And yet, if Mercy had been living as different insects for many lifetimes, then surely her final conclusions weren't based—or probably even influenced—by the squirrel and bee who happened to find her when she was ready to finish her mission and return home.

If Witch-Hazel were in charge of the choice, she wondered, what choice would she make? Let magic drain from the world? Fight to protect it?

She glanced at the gleaming gems grown into Fish-Breath's body, keeping him alive after the snake's zombie army had nearly killed him, and she worried about what the cost might be of fighting to protect magic.

From what she'd seen of magic, she wasn't sure it was worth protecting. Nothing was worth losing Fish-Breath again.

21

AFTER TOURING the grounds and finishing catching each other up, Fish-Breath and Witch-Hazel were reluctant to finish their stroll. Paw in paw, they walked slower and slower, trying to avoid returning to the throne room where they might have to face the All-Being or the turbines where they'd definitely have to face Twiggy.

They wandered through the hedge maze twice, following different paths; looped around the rose garden three times; and finally found themselves wending through an orchard of fruit trees. Their ivory branches were heavily laden with golden apples, silver pears, and bright copper oranges, nestled among the snowy leaves.

Witch-Hazel didn't feel the boundless, unmeasurable happiness that she'd imagined feeling upon being reunited with Fish-Breath, but she felt an easiness. A simple and pure contentment. Like everything was okay again, for the first time in a long time, and maybe, just maybe, it would keep being okay if they could keep being together. If she could keep seeing his smile that lit up her life like the sun lit up the world.

Life felt like an endless night without him, and with him, it felt like the beautiful morning of a day sure to be filled with adventures.

In the middle of the fruit orchard, they came to a tree larger than the others, standing taller than all the fruit trees around. Instead of fruit, this tree was covered in flowers. It made Witch-Hazel think of the magnolia tree where she and Zwi had found the Star Sliver hidden, deep underground. Except the tulip-like flowers here were every color imaginable, as if the pearlescent tree were a giant prism, and its ivory leaves dispersed the sunlight from all around into shards of rainbow.

Witch-Hazel heard a buzzing and called out, "Zwi? Is that you? Are you in this magnificent tree?"

A bee did come buzzing out of the tree, zigging and zagging in a beautiful, rhythmic dance that almost conjured music to Witch-Hazel's ears to match it. But the bee couldn't be Zwi; she was larger, longer in the abdomen, and her thorax was blacker while the dark stripes on her abdomen faded to a pale honey shade, almost translucent. She was a queen.

Witch-Hazel had never seen a honeybee queen before—they generally stayed in their hives. But she'd heard Zwi describe her hive's queen often enough.

"I'm sorry," Witch-Hazel said, "I thought you were my friend, Zwi. She's been looking for a new tree for her hive to move to, and if this one weren't taken, I think she would have loved it."

Witch-Hazel didn't know how Zwi would have felt about living in an ethereal ivory tree, growing on a cloud, beside a castle in the sky. But … she would definitely love the rainbow flowers.

"Witch-Hazel," the bee buzzed, and her buzzing really did sound like Zwi's, "it's me. I'm Zwi." She landed on a snowy white leaf with pointed edges, like a maple leaf. Other leaves on the tree were shaped differently, shaped like every kind of leaf Witch-Hazel had ever seen on a tree, as if this tree were every kind of tree unto itself. The All-Tree, flora counterpart to the All-Being.

"But …" Witch-Hazel tried to object, but her objections stuck in her throat.

The way this bee's antennae moved, tracing small circles, and her front legs pawed nervously at the leaf; the way her obsidian eyes gleamed—they were all so familiar. In spite of the changes, Witch-Hazel knew she was looking at her friend.

"You're a queen," Witch-Hazel said softly, almost afraid to give voice to the words. They sounded in her ears like the beginning of goodbye, and she wasn't ready to say goodbye to Zwi. Not yet. "You've been transformed."

Everyone was changing. Except Witch-Hazel.

"Is this your tree?" Witch-Hazel asked. "The one you've been looking for?"

Zwi bowed her head and fluttered her translucent wings in a way that made Witch-Hazel think she would have preferred to dance her answer, rather than be forced to buzz it for a squirrel who didn't speak her most native language. "Mercy showed me a vision in an amber mirror, like the one you described. My old hive has moved on. They live in a peach tree now, and they're doing fine. It's not a blessed tree, but they seem happy."

Witch-Hazel smiled sadly. She had expected as much. The hive couldn't have waited this long without doing anything to protect themselves from their tree dying. "Are you okay with that?" she asked.

Zwi nodded her triangular head. "Yes, it was the right thing for them." She spoke so much less formally now than when Witch-Hazel had met her. She'd changed while they'd travelled together.

Witch-Hazel had changed her. And so had Mercy.

"Mercy gave me a choice—I could go back to my hive, or …"

"Become a queen and stay here, in the clouds," Witch-Hazel said, saving her friend from having to say the words herself. "You're staying here."

Zwi flittered her wings and lifted off of the leaf. It swayed buoyantly at the loss of her slight weight—weightier now than when she'd been a worker. The new queen pirouetted and corkscrewed in the air above Witch-Hazel's head, dancing a waltz the squirrel would never understand.

"I've already built a basic nursery and laid the eggs for my first workers in the crotch of the tree. Me! Laying eggs!"

Witch-Hazel peered through the snowdrift's worth of leaves and saw a small, perfect cluster of hexagons where the tree's ivory trunk split into four heavy branches. Honeycomb in heaven.

"I'm happy for you," Witch-Hazel said. And she was, but she was also sad. Unlike Zwi, she couldn't stay here. This wasn't a home for a squirrel. At least, not this squirrel.

Witch-Hazel squeezed Fish-Breath's paw, and tried not to think about the hard, cool lump of Moon Opal on his webbed knuckle. He was more angelic creature than otter now. But he couldn't stay here. He couldn't.

When Witch-Hazel left here, she didn't want to leave alone. She had come here with friends—she might leave with different friends, but she couldn't bear the idea of traveling back down the beanstalk all by herself, leaving Fish-Breath behind.

"We should check in with Twiggy," Witch-Hazel said.

"Wait …" Zwi flew down and landed on the leaf again, causing it bob up and down on its stem. "The dance I was doing, just now …"

"It looked like a waltz," Witch-Hazel said. "It was lovely. Did it mean something? I'm sorry I never learned to read your dances …"

"It was a dance about you," Zwi said, "our travels together, our journey, *our friendship*. I told you once, ages ago, that one day my hive would dance dances about you. I promised you that, and I meant it. My workers will dance that waltz, and you will be remembered forever by honey-bees in the sky, pollinating ivory trees that grow golden apples and silver pears."

Witch-Hazel's eyes filled with tears of joy. She wanted to hug her friend, but even as much larger as she was now, the bee was much too small. Instead, she took an awkward step, letting her paw swing wide, spinning herself into a pirouette of her own. She spun about, shifting from one foot to the other, in a dance set to the music that had played in her head when she saw Zwi waltzing.

The queen bee flew down from her leaf and spiraled around the dancing squirrel. They danced together, waltzing or jigging, or just shimmying. Witch-Hazel didn't know much about dancing, but she did her best to pour all of her feelings of love and friendship—all of her hopes for Zwi's future and sadness at not being there to see it herself—into her shuffling feet and twirling tail.

Eventually, Fish-Breath began clapping his front paws and stamping his feet, providing them with a rudimentary rhythm and a tuneful but artless humming.

Witch-Hazel would have lived in that moment for-ever, but moments pass on, and the dance came to an end.

Witch-Hazel bowed to the queen bee, holding her tail in front of her like the skirts of a fancy ballgown. The queen bee did not bow back, but then, she was a queen now. Royal, regal, and part of the All-Being's court.

Fish-Breath took Witch-Hazel's paw again, and without even discussing it, they headed back toward the throne room of the All-Being's castle.

Twiggy was already there, looking indignant, practically shaking with anger and slapping her wide tail on the floor dramatically. Witch-Hazel didn't think she'd have the courage to address the All-Being, resplendent on her throne and staring with a plethora of eyes, with such vehemence. But then, Witch-Hazel didn't care about the machinery behind the endless rivers the way Twiggy did.

"There has to be another way!" Twiggy insisted. "The machine works perfectly. I've never seen such an ingenious machine before, and it deserves to work. It can't be right for a turbine of such … infinite perfection … to turn uselessly, devoid of water. If all it needs to return to its former glory, making the endless rivers loop from ground to sky, is for the cracks in the Sun, Moon, and North Star to heal, then surely you can heal them!"

The All-Being lifted a talon and examined the curled claws on it before they shimmered and turned into a fish's fin. "Yes, I can heal the Sun, Moon, and North Star with the Celestial Fragments stolen from them by the King of the Earthen Realm. I've told you that."

"Not like that!" Twiggy cried.

The All-Being shrugged, arms shimmering and turning into wings, and wings shimmering and turning into hoofed legs. Several new tails sprouted up behind her, and others disappeared. "Your otter friend cannot live without the Celestial Fragments. I can heal the broken Celestial Bodies with them, but I'd have to remove them from his body. Make your choice."

This was exactly what Witch-Hazel had feared.

Fish-Breath's tawny wings clamped firmly against his back.

Bravely, Witch-Hazel stepped forward and asked, "What do you mean, it's her choice?"

"Hers, yours, his …" The All-Being shrugged again. "It's your world. You have to choose."

Mercy took flight from where she'd been perched on the arm of the All-Being's throne. She floated through the air toward them and then stopped to hover. She sang, "I spent lifetimes in your world, and I've seen how magic can be hoarded, hidden away behind hierarchies, and used for evil. But I've also seen how it can be beautiful, connecting parts of the world that would otherwise stay far apart, giving hope to those who would use it for good. Magic is a double-edged sword, and I think that those who live in the world with that sword must decide whether it's worth wielding."

"If it costs Fish-Breath's life, then no," Witch-Hazel said with a simple finality. She couldn't believe Twiggy was even hesitating.

How dare she hesitate?

But then Witch-Hazel glanced up at Fish-Breath, standing nearly twice her height. He seemed hesitant too.

"How can you consider this?" Witch-Hazel asked, horrified. "Your life is worth so much more than *magic*." She spat the word "magic," as if it were the dirtiest of all curse words. "You're worth so much more than some stupid rivers!"

"My whole life," Fish-Breath said, placing the words calmly in the air, like laying out a pattern with pretty stones on the dry ground beside a stream bed, "I've planned with Twiggy that we'd come up here and fix the rivers. Since we were a pup and kit together. Since we were rock-hopping down Salisha Stream, skipping stones and skipping school. And now … I can fix them. Not Twiggy with her cleverness and knowledge, but me."

Witch-Hazel could hear in the otter's voice that he felt useless beside his cleverer friend, but she felt that way too. It didn't mean that either of them needed to sacrifice their lives. "You are worth more than the rivers," she repeated. She took his webbed paws, avoiding touching the gems on his knuckle and wrist that plagued him like cancer. They were beautiful tumors, trying to drag him down. "You are funny and fun. You can cook a gourmet meal out of scraps of dried debris in my backpack. You are brave and bold. And you do not need to make this sacrifice. I *gave* the Celestial Treasures to you. They're *yours*. Don't give them back."

"They were stolen—"

Fish-Breath began, but Witch-Hazel cut him off.

"No, they were *found. I found them, and I gave them to you*."

Fish-Breath looked lost. He glanced away from Witch-Hazel, seeming to search for an answer from Twiggy, Mercy, or even the All-Being. But Twiggy couldn't make eye contact, not after how ready she'd been to let her oldest friend give himself up for a few magical rivers. Mercy's butterfly face was inscrutable, and the chimerical All-Being defied interpretation.

Witch-Hazel looked down at his paws, still clutched in hers. She hated the Moon Opal on his knuckle and the Star Sliver on his wrist. They gleamed at her, twinkling and winking, as if they laughed at the worries of a mere squirrel and the heart she'd given to an otter.

The Celestial Treasures had dragged Witch-Hazel through dungeons, labyrinths, and illusions ... They'd nearly gotten her killed far too many times. But they'd also brought her and Fish-Breath together.

"Finding the Celestial Treasures and giving them to you is the best thing I've ever done," Witch-Hazel said, still looking at their paws joined together. "The only thing

I've ever done that feels worthwhile. *Keep them.* Please. Don't give them away."

"Don't say that," Fish-Breath said. He pulled a webbed paw free from hers and used it to turn her face back up toward his. "You traveled with Zwi, helping her achieve her dream of a hive in an All-Being blessed tree, and you rescued Mercy from having her egg destroyed again."

Twiggy chimed in, saying, "And you saved me from climbing up this beanstalk with no plan for handling the thin air. I might have asphyxiated if not for you, too stubborn to give up but without any air lilies."

Witch-Hazel cracked a smile. She could picture that. "You are stubborn," she agreed.

Twiggy laughed too, making her teeth whistle.

The All-Being interrupted, her voice singing like a choir: "This is not a decision that needs to be made today."

She was an immortal creature, and immortal creatures always have time.

Mercy added, "If you choose to stay here while deciding, I can induct each of you into my court. The Air Realm has long been neglected, and I'll need to fill my court here again."

"Your court is here?" Witch-Hazel asked. "In the All-Being's castle?" She did not want to live in the sky.

"In the valleys and the hills of the clouds here, yes," Mercy sang in her voice like a sailing flute solo. She gestured at Witch-Hazel and then Twiggy with her long, magenta leg. "I could grant each of you butterfly wings, temporary ones, of course, so you could fly through my realm with your friend while you all decide."

Twiggy's eyes widened, but Witch-Hazel shook her head decisively. She'd been invited by the queen of the Fire Realm to join her court and turned down the offer before. She didn't belong in the Air Realm any more than the Fire Realm. "We don't belong here," she said.

Twiggy sputtered, clearly longing for those butterfly wings. Witch-Hazel had to admit, they would make lovely accessories to the sundresses the stylish beaver always wore.

"I admit it's unusual for a beaver or a squirrel to join the Air Realm," Mercy said. "But I like the unusual."

Witch-Hazel looked at Fish-Breath and Twiggy imploringly. "Don't you remember our plans? You were going to go home to Riverton, and show me all around, show me all the places you've talked about. Don't you want to go home? Isn't that part of the point of an adventure? Returning home …"

Fish-Breath flapped his wings, as if to say, "But what about these things?"

Witch-Hazel shrugged. "So you have wings. So what?"

"They'll definitely stand out in Riverton," Twiggy said drily.

Now Fish-Breath laughed—a deep belly laugh that shook his whole body, causing him to double over forward and flap his wings.

"Does that matter?" Witch-Hazel asked archly.

"No," Fish-Breath said, sobering up quickly. "Except for the part where I only have them because of this broken off bit of the North Star in my wrist." With one paw, he pointed to the glittering diamond embedded in the wrist of the other.

"So, we don't tell anyone," Witch-Hazel said, feeling bristly and defensive. Both the angelic otter and stolid beaver gave her withering looks. "Okay, okay, so the wings will raise questions."

Fish-Breath crossed his arms. "I don't want to be walking around my hometown being the physical embodiment of why none of my neighbors can ever go on a pilgrimage to meet their All-Being. *I've been here.* What right do I have to deny them the same journey?"

"What right do they have to demand that journey at the cost of your life?" Witch-Hazel countered.

"Maybe they don't," Fish-Breath agreed. "But that doesn't mean I can't be generous. This magic isn't mine—"

Witch-Hazel tried to object, but Fish-Breath charged on.

"—if the mouse king stole these gems, they're not mine to keep. I don't feel right being the end of all magic in the world, just so I can go on living."

"What's so good about magic!" The echoes of Witch-Hazel's outburst taunted her with their irony. Fish-Breath was the proof of the good of magic. He was standing in front of her, because magic had saved him.

"Perhaps I can provide an alternative," the All-Being said.

22

"TIME PASSES DIFFERENTLY in these halls," the All-Being explained, "than in the world below. That's why the rest of you spent months on adventures and growing ... while the good otter did nothing more than examine a machine beyond his ken and send a few dream visions, guiding you here."

Witch-Hazel remembered only one dream vision—when Fish-breath had led her to the air lilies. She wondered if that meant she was forgetting some ... perhaps she really had danced with him during the revelry after Carnelian and Harvey's imaginary wedding? Or ...

Witch-Hazel caught Twiggy's eye, and she thought she saw the beaver's small round ears flick. But they were very small and hard to read emotions on. If Twiggy had beheld dream visions of Fish-Breath leading her here, then those were secrets for her to keep.

"You do not have to stay here while you decide the fate of the world." The All-Being shifted in her throne, rearranging countless paws, hooves, wings, and tails. "You can return to the world below, and as long as the Celestial Fragments are returned to the sky upon the otter's death—

or sooner, if you find another way—the damage can still be repaired."

"Another way?" Witch-Hazel asked. The words felt like a pivot, the kind of moment that changes your life, and even though it's only a few words, the change can't be taken back.

"The mouse king stole them," Mercy offered. "He might know a way to remove them without harming the otter host."

"Perhaps there's a surgeon who could save you!" Twiggy exclaimed. "If medicine did the work that the Fragments are doing, then you wouldn't need them anymore."

"Perhaps," Fish-Breath agreed tepidly. But then he looked at Witch-Hazel.

The otter and squirrel held each other's eyes for a long time, just looking at each other. Witch-Hazel wasn't sure that she believed another path could be found to saving Fish-Breath, but she didn't care. If he was willing to spend longer walking this path, searching fruitlessly for another, she would take that. She would take all the time with him that she could get. If they spent that time searching for medical geniuses or thieving mouse kings, then so be it. As long as she was with Fish-Breath, she would be happy. The only question was: would he be?

Fish-Breath smiled. That was answer enough.

Witch-Hazel hazarded, "I think, maybe, it's time we go on a new adventure?" Her tail flipped behind her, betraying her own excitement.

"Yes," Fish-Breath agreed, wholeheartedly this time. "I'm up for a new adventure."

Twiggy smiled too and said, "My hot air balloon is waiting."

About the Author

Mary E. Lowd is a prolific science-fiction and furry writer in Oregon. She's had nearly 200 short stories and a dozen novels published, always with more on the way. Her work has won numerous awards, and she's been nominated for the Ursa Major Awards more than any other individual. She is also the founder and editor of Zooscape. Learn more at marylowd.com.

The Original

DUNGEON SOLITAIRE
Tomb of Four Kings

Still Available for Free

at

matthewlowes.com/games

Complete Rules
are Print-Ready and Playable
with any Standard Deck
of Playing Cards

Complete Rulebook
&
Labyrinth of Souls Tarot Deck

Available at

matthewlowes.com/games

Labyrinth of Souls Fiction
Twelve books available now!

coming soon
Aftermath by Cynthia Coate-Ray

For more information, visit
shadowspinnerspress.com